BLUE SKY, BUTTERFLY

JEAN·VAN·LEEUWEN

BLUE SKY, BUTTERFLY

Dial Books for Young Readers
New York

Published by Dial Books for Young Readers
A Division of Penguin Books USA Inc.
375 Hudson Street
New York, New York 10014

Library of Congress Cataloging in Publication Data
Van Leeuwen, Jean.
Blue sky, butterfly / by Jean Van Leeuwen.
p.   cm.
Summary: When her father leaves, Twig feels isolated from
her older brother and her mother as they all try to
cope with the change in their lives.
ISBN 0-8037-1972-8 (trade).
[1. Divorce—Fiction.   2. Family life—Fiction.]
PZ7.V3273Bl   1996   [Fic]—dc20   95-34511   CIP   AC

For my father,
who gave me gardening

1

Midnight, and Twig should have been sleeping.

She was curled in the proper position, on her right side facing the wall. The quilt that Grandma Rose had given her when she was born, soft with age, was wrapped snugly around one shoulder. But her eyes were wide open. And there was a squeezed feeling, like a hard knot, in the center of her forehead.

It had been like this ever since her father had left. Thirteen days.

Twig listened. Faintly, from behind his always-closed door, came the thumping sound of her brother's guitar. A low, tuneless strumming, slightly off-key. Nathan was hardly ever home now, but when he was, this was what came from his room. Over and over, exactly the same, for hours. It was enough to drive you bananas, her father would have said.

Her eyes were like jack-in-the-boxes. As many times as she closed them, they popped right open again. "12:09," said the red numbers on the clock radio reproachfully. Time to be asleep so you can get up for school in the morning.

It was no use. Maybe if she had a glass of milk, it would help her feel sleepy.

Twig sat up. Icy January air streamed in the barely open window, making her shiver as she felt for her bathrobe at the bottom of the bed. Her bare feet hit cold wood floor.

Padding past her brother's door, she stopped to listen. *Strum, strum.* Something was definitely wrong with what he was doing. "The fingering," her friend Annie, taking violin for the third year, probably would have said. He ought to have taken lessons, not tried to teach himself. Just as she thought this, she heard a strange sound, like a yelp, behind the door. Something crashed loudly, and there was silence.

Maybe he broke the guitar, Twig thought. She felt guilty then, as if Nathan could see her through the door spying on him. Quickly she tiptoed past, down the stairs.

The downstairs was all dark. Where was her mother? From the tiny den near the front door came low talking sounds, a flickering light. She was watching TV again. Her mother never used to watch TV at all, and now she spent every night in the den, lying motionless on the broken-down brown couch. One time Twig had found her there in the morning, asleep in her clothes with the TV still on, the announcer talking earnestly about traffic tie-ups on Route 287.

Should she say something to her mother? Twig stood, uncertain, in the shadowy living room. If she did, if she told her she couldn't sleep, would her mother reach out a hand the way she used to and say, "Tell me where it hurts, sweetie," and come upstairs to sit on Twig's bed? Or would she just look up blankly, staring through her like she would a pane of glass? Her mother seemed to have gone somewhere too, since her father left. Shut herself up in a box with the opening pulled in after her.

Twig kept going, to the kitchen. She snapped on the light and right away the house felt warmer, friendlier. She reached into the refrigerator for the milk carton.

Thump, thump. A tail wagged against the floor.

"Hey, Charley." There was someone in the house to talk to.

Twig poured milk into her favorite mug, the one with the rabbits turning somersaults that she'd had since she was a baby. She reached for the oatmeal-cookie bag on the shelf, and took it and the mug to the table. Charley looked at her from his raggedy dog pillow by the back door, his yellow plume of a tail wagging.

"Want a cookie?"

The magic word brought him to his feet. Charley and her mother were supposed to be on diets, but no one cared about that anymore either.

Twig broke a cookie into small pieces. Charley rested his head on her knee, waiting, his tail still wagging. His warmth felt good. She fed him the cookie slowly to make it last longer. Then she rubbed his soft ear the way he liked. His mouth opened in a silly doggy smile.

"Good old Charley."

They sat that way a long time. Twig found herself wishing that the moment never had to end.

"Hey, Charley! I have an idea." She stood up, closed the cookie bag, and took her rabbit mug to the sink. He looked at her questioningly. "Come on. You can sleep in my room with me."

This had never been allowed. But she was sure her mother wouldn't notice.

"Come on, boy." Twig patted her knee.

Charley just sat there, his tail quivering. Then he walked over to his dog pillow, turned in a circle, and lay down, looking at the door.

He was her father's dog. He was still waiting for him to come home.

Slowly Twig rinsed out her mug and turned off the light. She walked upstairs, past the faint laughter of the TV, past her brother's door. He was strumming again. Apparently the guitar was still in one piece.

It felt strange, the house did, as if each of the rooms had broken off into islands.

2

The telephone was always ringing.

Her mother wasn't there to answer. She went for long walks, from which she returned with her cheeks spotted bright pink and her eyes shiny. Or she was out in the car, doing errands she said, though most days she forgot to stop by the grocery to pick up something for dinner. Or if she was in the house, shut up in her little office where she had been working for as long as Twig could remember on a book about the Middle Ages, she didn't seem to hear the phone.

Her brother was never home either. Basketball practice took all of Nathan's time, just as soccer had during the fall. And she had the feeling he was also hanging out at his friend Ben's house or his friend Todd's house, just to avoid coming home.

That left Twig to answer the persistent ring. She didn't want to. It was bound to be her father or Grandma Ruthie, and she didn't want to talk to either one of them.

Actually, it was easy if it was her father. She just hung up the phone without saying a word. She had already done it several times. She was so angry with him, she knew she would never speak to him again for the rest of her life. Still, she hated hearing his voice, that soft, almost pleading tone she'd never heard before. "Twig, is that you, honey? Don't hang up, please. I know you're angry, but I need to talk to you." She would feel suddenly as if she couldn't breathe, and for minutes after she slammed down the receiver, her hands wouldn't stop shaking.

Grandma Ruthie was another problem. She lived far away, out on the West Coast, and she was worried. She kept calling to find out how they were doing. Twig didn't know what to tell her. If she told the truth, "Not too good, Grandma," you couldn't tell what Grandma Ruthie might do. She might come swooping down out of the sky to take care of them. And Twig definitely did not want that.

Swooping down out of the sky was what she always thought of when she thought of this grandmother. Her other grandmother, Grandma Rose, her father's mother who had died three years ago, had been the kind who read stories and baked cookies and knitted sweaters with heart-shaped buttons down the front. But this one did none of those things. Twig didn't think she even knew how to cook. Mostly what Grandma Ruthie did was fly off to places, faraway places that Twig had never heard of even in social studies. Like Kuala Lumpur and Nepal and the Galápagos Islands, where no one lived except turtles and giant lizards. She sent them a lot of postcards, pictures of volcanoes and icebergs, strange-looking temples, yaks, and polar bears. And every once in awhile, without warning, she would drop in personally on her way from here or there. They would go meet her at the airport and Grandma Ruthie would be loaded down with bags, laughing and talking nonstop. She would stay for a day or two, telling stories that seemed too crazy to be true about climbing an Alp in a snowstorm or crossing the desert on a camel named Fred. And then Grandma Ruthie would be off again, into the sky.

She didn't really know this grandmother, that was the thing. And Grandma Ruthie was so busy with all her traveling. What good could she be to them now? So Twig told her that things were just fine. Her mother was doing well. She was out right now, but she would call as soon as she got back. Well then, as soon as Grandma Ruthie got back from Alaska.

The only person Twig wanted to talk to on the phone was her friend Annie. She and Annie had been friends since nursery school. Annie was so normal, with her two parents and her two funny little brothers and her cat and her bird, all living together in their tiny messy white house. In Annie's family something was always going wrong, but it was all right because they just laughed about it. Annie had the funniest laugh, like a wheezing chicken, her father said. She was the only one in the entire world right now who could make Twig smile.

So the two of them had worked out a telephone plan. "I'll call you at 5:32 P.M.," Annie would tell her at school. Or "At exactly 7:59 we will discuss the math homework." That way when the phone rang at 5:32 or 7:59, Twig didn't have to worry about answering it.

It was a relief to hear Annie's voice imitating Mr. Girardi, their math teacher, with a laugh bubbling just beneath the surface. "Students, if you please, we will now turn to page sixty-three in our mathematics books." Twig would feel her mouth twitch irresistibly into a smile.

Except for the day when the telephone rang at 5:14 P.M., just the moment Annie had said she would call. I can be funny too, thought Twig, picking it up.

"Twenty-seven chickens, twelve pigs, and nine dozen eggs."

The laugh she was expecting didn't come.

"Students, I am disappointed. Are you looking at Problem Twelve?"

Nothing but silence.

Then, "Twig, is that you?"

She couldn't believe it. "Daddy," she blurted out before she could stop herself.

"Honey," his voice went on, in that new urgent way. "I really want to see you. How would it be if we went out for dinner tomorrow night, just the two of us? Please, Pearl."

Pearl was his special name for her. Short for "Pearl of a girl."

"Don't call me that," she croaked. Her throat was closing up. She felt as if she were choking.

"I'm sorry."

"Don't," she whispered, and hung up the phone.

Then she was crying, huge hiccuping sobs that went on and on, until her head and stomach and everything else in between felt like one enormous ache.

3

The thing to do, thought Twig, was get rid of things.

Anything that reminded her of her father—out it would go. That was the way to start over, fresh and clean.

So she began piling them up on the bed: the tennis racket that they had picked out together, the camera he'd given her last Christmas, books, the special architect's paper he always brought home from his office, a set of mechanical pencils, a drawing he'd made of her room at its messiest, the hat he'd bought her on their trip to Disney World when she was six.

She hesitated over the framed picture of the four of them that sat on top of her bureau. It was her very favorite. They were sitting around the picnic table in the backyard, and they were laughing about something. Probably the burgers with all the crazy toppings that her father loved to cook on the barbecue. Grandma Ruthie had taken that picture just last summer. They looked like the happiest family in the history of the world. Nothing could break up that family.

"Ha!" said Twig loudly, and stacked it on the pile.

Then there was the locket. Another present from her father, this one from a business trip to California when she was little and didn't want him to go. "I'll bring you something," he had promised, and he had. She had been wearing the silver locket with its tiny picture of him inside ever since.

The locket was like part of her. She put it on automatically every morning, just after she brushed her teeth. Not anymore, she thought. Now she couldn't stand to look at it. On top of the pile it went.

Twig looked around the room. That seemed to be everything. She picked up the pile and started downstairs. What a relief to toss all this in the garbage, to eliminate her father from her life just as he had eliminated them from his.

At the garbage pail, though, poised with the lid in her hand, she stopped. Maybe it was years of her mother's training. You didn't just throw out valuable things like tennis rackets and cameras and jewelry. It was wasteful. On the other hand, you could give them away. She continued down the steep steps to the basement. Next to the furnace was a row of bags of outgrown clothes that her mother was planning to take to the hospital thrift shop. Twig dumped her pile into a half-full bag.

That was that. She went upstairs feeling lighter, as if she had just taken off a heavy, damp winter coat. It was working. Her room looked different, pared down, almost neat. Surprisingly, she even felt like cleaning it up.

A half hour later she had finished the job, sweeping all the clothes on the floor into piles, putting some back in her closet and the rest in the laundry. There. She had done it. Not the slightest trace of her father was left. Twig was ready to start her life over.

It occurred to her then that there was one thing left: her name.

Twig wasn't her real name. Christina was. It was her father who had first started calling her Twig, back in first grade. Ever since she was a baby, he had made up silly names for her, like Pearl and Mandy Sue and Rosie O'Grady. And once in awhile, for no reason she could ever figure out, Herb. Up until first grade she had been a chubby, round-faced little girl. But at six she had suddenly sprouted up, thin as a stick.

"Just look at that little wrist," her father had said, laughing, circling it with two of his big fingers. "It's like a twig."

The name had stuck. No one except Grandma Rose had called her anything else since then. Even the teachers at school called her Twig.

It had to go, she decided. Just this last thing and she would be free.

At dinner that night, one of those strange silent dinners with the three of them sitting together eating their frozen ravioli, their minds in three different places, Twig said, "I decided something today. I don't want to be called Twig anymore. From now on, my name is Christina. Okay?"

Her mother nodded absently. She wasn't really eating, Twig noticed, just pushing the tomato sauce around her plate. Had her face always been so thin? she wondered suddenly. And when was the last time she'd washed her hair?

Before she realized what she was doing, Twig said, "Finish your ravioli," just as if she were the mother and her mother the child.

Nathan was staring at her. "I thought you always liked that name."

"I did," said Twig. "But now I don't. It's silly. Christina is much more grown-up."

"Okay, then," Nathan answered agreeably. "Christina it is."

It was as easy as that. Only it wasn't, because people kept forgetting.

"Twig—I mean Christina," Nathan would say. "That sounds so fancy. How about Chris?"

Her teachers at school got it right most of the time, but not the kids. Especially Annie, who never liked things to change.

"Twig—oops, Christina," she kept saying. "Sorry, Twig. Oops, Christina." Until after awhile, some of the boys started calling her by a new name.

Twigoops.

It really was not easy changing your name.

4

She had a dream.

Coming home from school, Twig opens the back door to find the house empty. "Mom!" she calls. "Nathan! Where are you?" Her voice echoes in the stillness. But no one answers. Not even Charley comes to meet her, toenails clicking across the kitchen floor. She wanders from room to room: kitchen, living room, hall. That is when she begins to notice things. No coats are hanging on the wall pegs by the back door. No food is in the refrigerator, no mail stacked up on the hall table. She opens the front closet and nothing is inside but a row of empty hangers.

It comes to her then in a sickening flash. They have moved away and left her behind.

Twig woke up, her forehead damp with sweat, her heart pounding. It was a dream, she told herself. Just a stupid dream. It wasn't real. Slowly her heart quieted to its normal beat.

But then another closet with nothing but empty hangers came creeping into her mind. And she was remembering the day her father left.

It had started out so ordinary, just an ordinary Sunday morning with her father making pancakes on the griddle. Hamburgers outside and pancakes inside: Those were his specialties. On St. Patrick's Day he put in green food coloring and on Easter he made pancakes in the shape of rabbits. But this Sunday the pancakes had been Twig's favorites, the ones with tiny bits of apple and nuts. Had he been sillier than usual that morning, making dumb jokes? Had her mother been quieter? Twig hadn't noticed anything at the time. It was only later, in the long dark gray afternoon with snow flurrying at the windows, that they had the talk.

It was the talk that all parents probably had with their children when they told them they were getting a divorce. It felt that way to Twig, not real but like a script they had rehearsed. Her father sat in his favorite dark blue chair, not slouched down comfortably as usual, but straight as a soldier. Her mother, feet tucked under her on the couch, face nearly hidden by the tall collar of her sweater, looked small. Already that day she seemed to be going away from them. Words came out of both their mouths stiffly, like characters in a play. Words like "haven't been getting along" and "grown apart" and "no one's fault." Her mother said that last one several times, as if it was important.

Twig couldn't look at them. Her eyes wandered out the window, following the fat swirling snowflakes that caught in the branches of the pine trees, and settled on the grass. Would they stick? she wondered, as she always did. Would there be school tomorrow?

"So we have decided to separate."

She had to look at her father then. He paused, blinked, cleared his throat. For a moment he seemed to have forgotten his lines. "Uh—this is what we've decided. I will be moving out, to an apartment. You children will stay here with your mother." His voice grew stronger. "I'll be nearby, though. We will still see each other. All the time, in fact. All you have to do is call me, and I'll be there. It will work out, you'll see."

He looked so earnest, they both did, willing them to understand. Nathan, looking at his knees, nodded, and so did Twig.

They kept on nodding, like puppets.

Inside, though, Twig did not understand. She didn't believe a word of it. People who got divorced were supposed to fight. But her parents got along fine. She had never even heard them raise their voices. Not one time. Her father traveled. Her mother spent hours shut up in her little office. But they seemed happy. They smiled and joked and went to her school concerts and Nathan's basketball games and sometimes out to dinner by themselves. At least they used to.

No, it couldn't be real.

The snow stopped. The next morning Twig went to school and everything was so normal: the Monday vocabulary test, tryouts for the spring play. It didn't seem as if the sky had fallen, so she decided it hadn't. It had all been a mistake. Her parents didn't mean it, they had just gotten angry about something. She hurried home after school, anxious to hear that everything had been patched up, even hearing the words her father would use. "Sorry, kid! Nobody's perfect, not even you and me."

She walked in the door and no one was there. Only Charley, napping in the narrow stripe of winter sun on the living room rug, too comfortable to get up to greet her. Upstairs, her mother's office door was closed. Twig wasn't supposed to disturb her when she was working. That was normal. Her father was at his office and her mother was writing.

Twig stood next to the door. No sound came from inside. Well, sometimes she just sat and thought. Twig started down the hall to her own room, stopped, then came back to her parents' bedroom.

Standing in the doorway, she felt like a witness to a natural disaster. A tornado had blown through, destroying half the room. Everything on the left side was gone: her father's tall bureau, his bedside table and reading lamp, the chair where he always left his ties draped like limp striped flags, even the pillow on his side of the bed. The closet where his suits had hung stood open, but nothing was inside. Nothing but a few bare hangers.

One, two, three, four, five, she counted. Like skeletons of suits. That was all he had left behind.

He was really gone.

Behind her she heard a step, and then Twig felt her mother's arms around her, squeezing her so tight that she couldn't speak or breathe or hardly think.

Why why why why why?

5

If only she could talk to her mother, it would help.

Twig had questions, unasked for so long now that she couldn't quite remember what they were. She felt worried all the time. She couldn't fall asleep at night, and when she did she kept having bad dreams. But Twig's mother had stopped talking. Since the day her father left, she had hardly said a word to anyone.

She drifted in and out of the house, ghostlike, here one minute and then gone. She seemed younger to Twig, dark hair pulled back from her pale face in an untidy ponytail, eyes large and lost-looking.

She didn't do the things a mother should do. She didn't cook anymore, except when she remembered to put the frozen dinners in the microwave. She didn't shop unless Twig or Nathan reminded her, and then she was likely to come back without half the things on the grocery list. She never did the laundry or the ironing or the cleaning. Fuzzy gray dustballs skittered across the wood floor when you opened the front door.

It wasn't right. It was making Twig extremely nervous.

She talked to Nathan about it one morning at breakfast. Her mother didn't get up to have breakfast with them anymore either.

"Yeah," he mumbled, spooning in great mouthfuls of cereal while she talked. "I know. It's weird."

His wrist was so thin to hold up such a big hand, she thought.

"But what are we going to do?" she persisted. "Who is going to take care of us?"

Nathan gazed at her through shaggy long hair. Usually her mother would have made him get a haircut by now. He looked uncomfortable, squirmy. Ever since he'd started high school, he didn't talk to Twig much. But she must have looked desperate, because then he said, "Hey, don't panic. She'll be okay." Nathan ran a hand through his hair, pushing it out of his eyes. "Probably she just needs to be left alone. You know, give it time."

He glanced at the kitchen clock, then jumped up.

"Gotta go. Time for my bus."

With half a doughnut in his hand and a moon of sugar around his mouth, he was out the door.

Time. If that was what her mother needed, Twig could give her that. Just wait patiently for her to become herself again.

Meanwhile, though, the house was falling apart. The dustballs had clumped together in furry piles under the piano. Sticky tomato sauce dishes were always stacked in the sink. Laundry was overflowing the wicker basket in the bathroom that she and Nathan shared.

Twig had pushed the dirty clothes down as far as she could, but they were spilling over the top again like a waterfall. And she didn't have another clean shirt for school tomorrow. Well, maybe she could do laundry.

She dragged the heavy basket downstairs to the laundry room. Okay. Now what?

Her mother divided the laundry into different loads, she remembered. On top were a bunch of Nathan's smelly basketball clothes. They ought to go in a separate load, she decided. She didn't want them touching her nice shirts and pants.

She didn't even want to touch them herself. But she had to. Holding each one gingerly by its edge, she piled them into the washer: T-shirts, sweatpants, shorts, socks. Just those made a full load.

Now to set the machine. All the buttons and dials were confusing. Large load, medium, small, miniwash. Hot water, warm, cold. Regular or gentle cycle. Nathan's clothes needed a lot of everything, she decided. Hot water, lots of soap, and a long, long wash.

She read the directions on the detergent bottle and poured in a brimming capful of pink stuff.

Twig closed the lid. The machine began to hum. Soon it was making satisfying splashing sounds.

That hadn't been so hard. She went upstairs to do her homework.

Half an hour later she came back to check. The washer had shut off, just as it was supposed to. Inside, the clothes were damp and squashed and smelled clean, just as they were supposed to. Great. Now for the dryer.

But as she picked up one of Nathan's T-shirts, she frowned. What was that smudge of blue on the sleeve? Had that been there before? Then she noticed that all the white things—socks, T-shirts, Nathan's favorite shirt from basketball camp—were tinged with blue.

Oh, no. Now she remembered. It was whites and darks. Those were her mother's separate loads.

Could she fix this? What would her mother do? Of course, she thought. Bleach.

Quickly Twig separated the whites and darks, tossing the darks into the dryer. She was starting to feel uneasy. What if Nathan came home and saw what she had done to his favorite shirt? And that all his white socks were now light blue? She had to hurry.

But you had to be careful with bleach. Twig

measured it out slowly, so nothing would spill on her or her clothes. Once her mother had ruined a red sweater she was wearing when the bleach had splashed.

She had the washer going again—that powerful bleach smell scouring away all the blue—and the dryer. Things were under control. She hoped.

Back to her homework. Then back downstairs to check the laundry.

The bleach had worked. The white socks were sparkling white again, and Nathan's basketball-camp shirt no longer had that blue streak at the bottom. Twig smiled with relief. Something seemed different about the shirt, though. She wasn't quite sure what. Oh, wow. The neck and sleeve edges and the lettering, which had been red, were now a strange orange.

Orange, the worst color! Twig hated it. So would Nathan.

And what was that burning smell? Something seemed to be on fire in the dryer.

Quickly Twig shut it off. Opening the door, she pulled out Nathan's basketball shorts. Or were they? They were made of the same shiny blue uniform material, but they were tiny, shrunk to the size of a handkerchief. Baby shorts.

This was terrible. This was a disaster.

"Hey, what's happening?"

Nathan stood in the doorway, frowning at the ruined shorts she held in one hand, the ruined shirt in the other. Snow dripped from his sneakers, making a spreading puddle on the floor.

Her mother hated that.

"I thought—I was trying—" She stopped, afraid she was going to cry.

"It's okay," Nathan said. "I've got other basketball clothes." He clomped to the refrigerator, took out the orange juice, and poured a huge glass.

"Hey, it's okay," he said again, his voice softening.

A new puddle grew by the refrigerator door.

6

Nothing was okay really.

And it kept getting worse. The weather didn't help. It was the coldest February on record, they said on TV. Gray and gloomy with little snowstorms every few days. The dining room roof leaked. Twig's father would have been on the phone or up on the roof, stopping it, but her mother looked without interest at the water dripping onto the honey-colored rug. Finally Nathan put a bucket under it.

She kept going for her walks, snowflakes fluttering around her head like a cloud of moths.

"Don't forget your mittens," Twig had to remind her, just as her mother always used to tell her. "You ought to wear a hat."

Twig didn't like being the mother. It felt odd.

She was so tired of frozen dinners, she could scream. The same ones over and over. And pizza and take-out from the Chinese restaurant. She found herself longing for the meals her mother used to make, things she hadn't even known she liked. Roast chicken. Meat loaf. Mashed potatoes. Broccoli.

In desperation one day she got out one of her mother's cookbooks. Maybe she could cook a meal. But all the recipes seemed so complicated. They used strange-sounding ingredients like leeks and artichokes, balsamic vinegar and tarragon leaves. Twig remembered the laundry and thought she'd better wait.

She was waiting for her mother to come back from wherever she was. Days went by. Weeks. On the first of March it rained, and her mother walked out into a fog thick as wool. Twig watched her disappear, like a small boat adrift on a great gray sea.

She needed to talk to Nathan again. But he no longer ate breakfast, just snatched a doughnut on his way out the door. And most nights when he came home from basketball, she had already finished her dinner. More and more he seemed to lead a secret life. When did he do his homework? she wondered. Did he ever study? Maybe not. A paper that fell out of his jacket onto the kitchen floor had a big red *F* on it. Could he actually be failing biology? He slipped in and out so quickly and quietly, she could never catch up with him to ask.

One afternoon Twig came home from school with a sore throat. It was the tickly kind, not yet really sore but on its way. The kind that needed a mother to take care of it.

Her mother's car wasn't in the driveway.

"I'm home," she called to Charley, as she let herself in the back door. He came ambling, stretching, into the kitchen.

If she was really sick in bed, her mother would always make tomato soup and bring it to her on a tray. If she had a bad sore throat, she would fix tea with honey. This sore throat wasn't quite that bad. Still, it needed something hot. Hot chocolate was what it needed.

Twig took down the cocoa, mixed it up with milk in a pan, and turned on the front burner. She stirred with a wooden spoon until the mixture was light brown and bubbling. Then, while it cooled a little, she went upstairs and changed into her sweatshirt with the hood. You had to be warm and cozy when you were sick.

Her mother was supposed to make her feel warm and cozy. She was supposed to fix the hot chocolate and then play cards with her at the kitchen table. That was what she always used to do. Those were the rules.

Blinking back a tear, Twig poured the hot chocolate into her rabbit mug and plopped a fat marshmallow on top. She carried it to the table. Then she got out the cards and laid out a game of solitaire.

"Come here, Charley."

She stroked his head, talking to him loudly so he wouldn't wander away and leave her alone.

"Red queen on black king. That's good. Black six on red seven. Oh look, Charley, the ace of clubs!"

Something moved outside. Twig looked up to see a basketball flying through the air. It bounced on the rim of the garage hoop and went through. Nathan's jacket moved underneath, retrieving it. That was unusual. Basketball practice must have been called off. She heard a voice, and saw his friend Ben standing next to the white mountain of snow at the edge of the driveway.

This was nice, like old times. The two of them used to spend hours out there shooting baskets.

"Listen to that," she said to Charley.

The bounce of the ball, the squeak of shoes. Grunts, a laugh, good-natured arguing.

It sounded so normal. For the first time in weeks something seemed normal. Charley wagged his tail. Twig felt herself smiling.

She poked her spoon down into her mug and lifted up the half-melted marshmallow. Slimy-sweet, it filled her mouth with warmth. This was her favorite part of drinking hot chocolate. She let it melt slowly until the last of its sweetness slid down her throat.

Charley whined. He was standing at the window looking out. It had grown suddenly quiet out there, Twig realized. Maybe they had quit and gone to Ben's house.

She heard a strange sound, like an animal, and she stood up. Nathan and Ben were scuffling over the ball, rolling around on the snow-smudged black asphalt. First one had it, then the other. Then it bounced away. But instead of getting up, laughing and punching each other on the arm as they usually did, they continued to struggle. Over and over they rolled, dark hair, red hair, an octopus of arms and legs, not making a sound.

Ben was bigger. He had to be stronger than skinny Nathan. But Nathan was acting as if some awful fury was inside him. Again and again he rolled and flailed, until somehow he was on top. His face was bright pink and he was breathing hard. She could see white puffs of breath in the cold air.

At last Ben lay still. Nathan sat astride his chest, his fist raised. The look in his eyes was like nothing Twig had ever seen. This wasn't Nathan.

Suddenly his arm went limp, falling to his side. Slowly he stood up. Ben stood too. Without saying anything, as if in a silent movie, he picked up his book bag and walked down the driveway.

Tears were running down Nathan's cheeks.

Twig couldn't watch anymore. Gathering up her piles of cards, she put them away. She took her empty mug to the sink and ran water in it until the foamy mud-brown water ran clear. Then she went upstairs.

The basketball bounced again in the driveway.

She swallowed. Her throat seemed worse.

Twig picked up the telephone and dialed Grandma Ruthie's number.

"Grandma," she said. "Please come."

7

Grandma Ruthie arrived by taxi.

She came sailing in, taking everyone by surprise, with an odd-looking tall fur hat on her head and four overflowing shopping bags.

"Mama!" said Twig's mother weakly, looking startled out of a dream.

"Yes, it's me." Grandma Ruthie thumped her on the back, smiling over her shoulder at Twig. "Just dropped in for a little visit."

Brisk, thought Twig. That was the word for Grandma Ruthie. It was one of her vocabulary words from last week. Tiny and bright-eyed, with a mass of flyaway gray hair, she was in motion all the time.

"Nathan, look at you! You're growing by leaps and bounds." She reached up on tiptoe to kiss his cheek. "Would you take all this stuff to my room? Oh, except for that bag. I brought you each something from Alaska. Twig, you can take this small one to the kitchen. It's Portuguese bread from my favorite bakery. Have you tried it? You'll like it, I know. I'd love some right now with a cup of tea."

They sat around the table while Grandma Ruthie emptied out her shopping bag, unwrapping fat balls of tissue paper.

"Black currant jam. Salmon jerky. Bull-kelp pickles. They're made from seaweed, you know. Delicious! Now this is for you, Nathan. It's a fossil from some ancient sea creature, I'm not just sure what. And for you, Twig, a whale's tooth."

It was long and cone-shaped, like the tip of a tusk. Where did Grandma Ruthie get it? she wondered. Did she reach right into the whale's mouth?

It wouldn't surprise her. Grandma Ruthie seemed to have done everything else in Alaska.

"After I visited the glacier," she told them over her cup of tea, "I was determined to get to the Arctic Circle. I was heading north by train. But storms kept delaying us, and then there was a moose on the tracks. So in Fairbanks I hired a bush pilot to take me by plane. And first thing you know, we're grounded by a blizzard. Three days of snow, up to the windows of the cabin I was staying in. My, it was cold. So then, would you believe it? I caught a ride the rest of the way by dogsled. Oh, that was fun!"

So much talk was making Twig's head spin. She wasn't used to it. Sitting there in the warm lamplight, she was suddenly aware that they were all together as they hadn't been for weeks—though Nathan looked like he'd been tied to his chair and would rather be somewhere else. And, miracle of miracles, her mother was smiling. A pale smile, but it was something.

She was glad Grandma Ruthie had come.

Twig's sore throat had turned into a cold, not too bad, but she was still sniffling. Grandma Ruthie noticed it the next morning.

"We can't have this," she pronounced sternly, as if she were in charge of colds. "I'll just make you a nice soup."

So Grandma Ruthie could cook after all. Most of that afternoon she chopped and stirred. Twig had never seen so many vegetables going into one pot.

"Uh, Grandma," Twig said when she saw the cabbage, "I don't really like vegetables that much."

Grandma Ruthie waved her hand, smiling. "You'll like this. It's Italian. It's called *ribollita*."

And amazingly, Twig did. So did Nathan, although he frowned when he encountered soggy bread in his bowl.

"It's a peasant soup," Grandma Ruthie explained. "Poor people put in all the scraps they had, even stale bread."

She had a story too about where she had gotten the recipe.

"I was on my way from Paris to Italy," she said.

"But then there was a railroad strike, and I found my-self stranded in the train station in a tiny Italian town in the middle of the night. Well, I happened to strike up a conversation with two nuns, Sister Sofia and Sis-ter Giuliana. Oh, they were lovely people. We sat on a bench talking half the night, and the next day they took me to their school for orphaned children and we had the most marvelous lunch. And they showed me the library at the school. Do you know, it was filled with manuscripts going all the way back to the fif-teenth century! Not locked up or under glass or any-thing. They let me hold one in my hands. It was just as it had been written by the monks hundreds of years ago, in faded brown ink. And when I left, they gave me this recipe."

Twig's mother dipped another spoonful of soup into her bowl, and Grandma Ruthie beamed.

"Remember, Carrie, when we first moved into our house and your father decided we needed a garden, and he kept digging until he'd dug up the whole backyard? And he'd say, 'Put the water on, Ruthie,' and when it was boiling, he'd run into the kitchen with fistfuls of just-picked beans."

Again came that tiny flicker of a smile. "He used to wash the tomatoes off with the hose," Twig's mother said dreamily, "and we would eat them right there in the garden. Still warm from the sun."

It was the most she had said in a very long time.

That night, going to the kitchen for a glass of milk, Twig saw that her mother and Grandma Ruthie were already there. They stood in the shadowy darkness next to the sink, their arms around each other. Maybe her mother was crying, she couldn't tell. For the longest time they stood that way, not moving or saying a word.

Twig turned and tiptoed quietly away.

Over the next few days Grandma Ruthie took charge. Twig was amazed. She came home from school to find the dustballs gone from the living room. Clean laundry was stacked in piles, waiting to be put away, and the refrigerator was full again. Dinners were an adventure. Grandma Ruthie cooked dishes from everywhere her "wandering feet," as she called them, had taken her. Chicken pie from Morocco, noodles and shrimp from Thailand, curry that set everyone's mouth on fire from India. And with every meal came a story.

"I was bicycling in the south of Spain," she began the night that Annie came for dinner. Annie didn't quite believe the stories Twig had been telling her. She wanted to hear one for herself. "And I'd brought along a picnic. I saw a nice spot at the side of a country road, so I sat in the shade of a tree and began eating my lunch. After awhile I had the strangest feeling, as if someone was watching me. I looked up and discovered that I was in a pasture, surrounded by cows. Not your ordinary mild-mannered milk cows, though. No, these were bulls."

Annie's eyes grew large in her head.

"Well," continued Grandma Ruthie, "I thought of bullfights, and was relieved that I wasn't wearing red. The bulls seemed calm enough, but as soon as I stood up, thinking I could sneak away, they moved closer. I considered climbing that tree, but I wasn't tall enough to reach the lowest branch."

She paused to pass the bull-kelp pickles. "They're seaweed," she told Annie. "Try one."

"No, thank you," said Annie and Twig together.

"Be brave, girls." Grandma Ruthie forked a thick slice onto each of their plates.

"So what did you do?" Twig prompted.

"I talked to them. First I used all the Spanish words I knew, but that didn't seem to impress them. So I switched to English. I told them how handsome they were. I complimented them on their fine horns and shiny coats. After awhile I began reciting Shakespeare and *Alice in Wonderland*, and poetry by Emily Dickinson. It was Emily who finally did it, I think. Put those bulls into some sort of poetic trance. And I tiptoed away."

Annie was still staring. "'The time has come,' the Walrus said, 'To talk of many things.' Did you recite that?" It was her favorite part.

"I did," answered Grandma Ruthie. "And I'm happy to say they liked it very much. It seemed to me they were swishing their tails. Made them a bit too frisky, though. That's when I decided to try Emily."

Annie and Grandma Ruthie smiled at each other across the table.

Quite by accident, Twig took a bite of bull-kelp pickle. Strange, it didn't taste like seaweed smelled. It was kind of like a pickled apple.

Not bad really.

8

Two days later Grandma Ruthie packed up her things.

Not yet, cried Twig inside her head. Oh, please. Not so soon.

But it was time for Grandma Ruthie's feet to wander. "I'm going spelunking," she told Twig. "In New Mexico."

"Spelunking?"

"Exploring caves. You know, stalactites, stalagmites. Communing with bats and other creepy creatures."

"Oh. Great, Grandma."

It felt as if they'd been on a merry-go-round for a week, with colored lights and music playing. Twig had seen her mother smile four times. It was getting to be a habit almost. But suddenly the merry-go-round stopped spinning and they had to get off.

What happened now? Surely Grandma Ruthie would tell them. She wouldn't just leave.

But she did. She strapped up her battered blue suitcase, plopped her fur hat crookedly on her head, hugged them all, and staggered through swirling snow to a waiting taxi.

"'Bye!" She waved a floppy mitten out the window.

Twig imagined her flapping her arms, shopping bags and all, and taking off into the sky. Grandma Ruthie didn't even need a plane. Talking would keep her up in the air. Before you knew it, she would swoop down out of the clouds in New Mexico. And by dinnertime she'd be talking to bats deep in some underground cave.

The thought made Twig smile.

But then the taxi turned the corner. In the space of an eye-blink, silence fell over the house. Twig's mother vanished into her study. Nathan slipped out the back door, to basketball or wherever it was he went. Charley curled up with a sigh on his dog pillow. The house was so quiet Twig could hear it creak, as if settling its bones for a long sleep.

Slowly she climbed the stairs to her room. Picking up the whale's tooth from her bookshelf, she held it smooth in her hand. Strange to be holding something that used to live underwater, chewing on fish or whatever whales did.

The quiet was painful. Twig couldn't bear it. She snapped on her radio, and country music twanged into the room.

Everything was just as it had been before Grandma Ruthie had come, she thought. Worse, really. Before, Twig had been used to the quiet. Not one time during her visit had Grandma Ruthie said anything about her father leaving. She hadn't even mentioned his name. She hadn't gotten Twig's mother to pull herself together and act like a mother again. Or Nathan to come home. She hadn't told them how they were supposed to go on.

All at once Twig felt furious with Grandma Ruthie. How could she just fly in and out like that? She was like a child herself.

Twig felt as if she were about a hundred years old.

She listened to someone bawling about careless love and someone else telling what she'd do to her man if he left her. A dull ache started in her throat, then sank slowly to her stomach, where it settled in to stay. Missing her father was like a stitch in her side that wouldn't go away.

After awhile she noticed the gray light fading at her window. Wearily she went downstairs to see what was left in the refrigerator for dinner.

The last of the Moroccan chicken was there in a pie plate. Enough for three if Nathan decided to come home. Twig took it out and noticed a note stuck on top: "Reheat 20–25 min. at 350°. Don't overcook!"

Well, at least they didn't have to have frozen dinners tonight. She looked to see what was in the freezer. Lined up below the ice cream were six foil-wrapped packages, all labeled, with heating directions in Grandma Ruthie's big scrawly writing.

Twig whistled. "Thank you, Grandma." She had left them something after all: food for a week.

And, surprisingly, Nathan came home for dinner. He left his wet basketball shoes at the door, and without saying anything, started setting the table.

Twig stared at his back until he turned around.

"What's wrong?" he asked.

"What's wrong with you?"

"Nothing. I'm helping with dinner, that's all."

Pink crept up his ears.

"When she mended my socks," Nathan mumbled, not looking at her, "Grandma kind of told me. My feet are as big as my dad's now, I better try on his shoes."

This was amazing, Twig thought, watching him pour milk into two glasses. This was good.

Then, while he went to call their mother, she thought of one of Grandma Ruthie's Alaska stories, the one about the northern lights.

"I was close to the Arctic Circle, so far north that the days were only four hours long. Can you imagine it? Twenty hours out of twenty-four of complete darkness. At first I was disappointed, since there was so much I wanted to see. But then, the second night, I looked up into that night sky and I saw colors. The most wonderful greens and yellows and whites, and later on reds and oranges. Fingers of flame seemed to be dancing up there, slowly changing patterns as if some great unseen fire was burning to the north. As I stood watching, I had the eerie feeling that the sky had come alive and I was part of it. It was the most mysterious, most glorious thing.

"It's strange, isn't it?" she said, her eyes looking across the table into Twig's. "Even the darkest night has its wonders."

9

The postcard came five days later.

It was addressed to Twig, and showed a very large stalactite and a very small person. On the back was scribbled, "Super spelunking! How about white-water rafting in Colorado in July? Love, Grandma."

Twig read it again. Was Grandma Ruthie really inviting her along on one of her adventures? Just her? Would she want to? She kind of wished Grandma Ruthie had left out the word "white-water."

She propped up the postcard next to the whale's tooth to think about it.

A few days after that, the package arrived. Small and square, this one was addressed to her mother. It sat waiting mysteriously all afternoon on the kitchen table.

"Oh, Mama," sighed Twig's mother, shaking her head, when she opened it.

Inside were three little packets of seeds: bush beans, carrots, and sugar snap peas.

"Mama, Mama," she repeated, then walked away, leaving the box on the table.

That was that, thought Twig. At dinnertime she stuffed it into a cupboard.

Snow melted into mud. The white mountain next to the driveway dwindled to a hill. Small green patches appeared, then spread in the front yard. Buds began to swell on the tips of tree branches. Winter was finally loosening its hold.

Basketball was over. Without a moment's pause, Nathan went right into track. He ran for hours after school, returning home with his hair pasted damp to his forehead, shirt hanging limply from his bony shoulders. Piles of clammy sweats covered his bedroom floor, then spread to cover every surface of the bathroom. Just when Twig decided she couldn't stand it another minute, he surprised her by gathering up the piles and taking them to the laundry room.

She heard the washer, and went to see.

"You mean you know how to do laundry?" she asked, astonished.

"What's there to know? Any dimwit can do it."

She picked up a soggy towel and threw it at him.

Nathan caught it, grinning, and slam-dunked it into the washer.

"Well, almost any dimwit."

She would show him, she thought. As soon as the water was sloshing and Nathan had gone upstairs, she went to the phone.

"Annie," she said, "how does your mom make her ziti?"

"I'll call you back," said Annie.

Since Grandma Ruthie's dinners had run out and they had gone back to frozen ones, Twig had been thinking about cooking. There was something satisfying about taking a little of this and a little of that, then mixing and stirring and tasting until you came up with something delicious. It had seemed simple when Grandma Ruthie did it. Maybe she could try. All you had to do, after all, was follow directions. One step at a time.

Five minutes later she had the recipe. It was always her favorite dinner when she ate over at Annie's. And she remembered Annie's mom saying it was the easiest thing in the world to make. Looking over the recipe, Twig saw that she was in luck. Everything she needed was in the house.

She took out all the ingredients: pasta, tomato sauce, spices, cheese. Grandma Ruthie always put everything out on the counter before she started so she wouldn't forget. "Cook pasta according to package directions," began the recipe. That was easy. Meanwhile, warm up the tomato sauce. Meanwhile, grate the two cheeses.

It was the meanwhiles that were hard. While she tried to grate the cheeses, scraping her knuckles instead, the tomato sauce was splashing all over the stove. While she was cleaning that up, the timer rang, meaning that the pasta was done. Twig ran to the recipe to see what came next. "Drain pasta." How did you do that? When you poured out the water, the noodles poured out too. And how were you supposed to do everything at the same time?

Slow down, she told herself. Then she remembered Grandma Ruthie holding a round silvery thing with holes, swishing around noodles while steam curled around her head like a wreath.

Twig drained and grated and layered everything into a casserole dish. She sprinkled a little extra cheese on top. It wasn't in the recipe, but that was what Grandma Ruthie did.

Finally it was ready for the oven.

She pulled over a chair and sat next to the oven door, watching until the noodles gently rose and fell and the cheese blurred, then bubbled. That meant it was done, the recipe said.

Carefully, with two potholders, she lifted it out. Amazing. It looked and smelled just like Annie's mom's ziti.

She set the steaming dish in the middle of the table, and called her mother and Nathan.

"This is it?" said Nathan, when she passed him his

plate. "This is the whole meal? Where are the vegetables and salad and rolls?"

Oh. His plate did look kind of bare with just a mound of ziti on it. Meanwhile, while you were making the casserole, you were supposed to be making all those other things to go with it.

"You could have a piece of bread," she said.

But her mother was taking a bite, lifting her fork to her mouth, chewing.

"Oh, my," she said. "You really made this?"

Twig nodded.

"It's delicious, sweetie." She was looking at Twig as if she really saw her. And smiling.

Smile number five.

10

Her father called again.

This time Twig didn't answer the telephone, Nathan did. She knew it was him, though, by the way Nathan acted. He sat tipped back in a kitchen chair, drinking orange juice and twisting and untwisting the phone cord while he grunted answers to questions.

"Yeah . . . Not bad . . . Okay." Just before he hung up, Twig heard him say, "All right. Seven."

"Seven what?" she asked.

Nathan drained his juice glass, looking at the ceiling. "O'clock."

"What's happening at seven o'clock?"

"Dad's picking me up."

"What? You can't do that, Nathan. You wouldn't."

His eyebrows knit together darkly. Just like her father's when he was angry, she thought. Sometimes, just for an instant, Nathan looked exactly like him.

"I'm having dinner with Dad, that's all. And seeing his apartment."

Banging down his chair, he walked past her, out the kitchen door.

Twig pursued him up the stairs.

"After what he did? How can you even talk to him?"

Abruptly Nathan turned to face her on the landing. "What are you talking about? It wasn't just him, you know. We have no idea what happened."

Twig could feel her voice rising, going out of control. "He left! That's what happened."

"Sure he left. Someone had to." He was scowling at her now, jaw tight, fists clenching and unclenching. "But it's not that simple. You've got to know that. Don't be a complete baby, Twig. Oh, this is such a mess!"

Without warning, one fist shot out and hit the wall. "Ow! Damn!"

"Are you all right?" Twig couldn't believe he'd done that.

He looked down at his hand, flexing the fingers, then slowly nodded. Without another word, he climbed the rest of the stairs to his room and shut the door.

Twig went back to the kitchen. A few minutes later she heard Nathan coming down again.

"Anyway," he said quietly, "he's still our father."

And he went out the door.

At seven o'clock the house felt hushed, expectant. Her mother was out, doing research at the college library, she'd said. Nathan was somewhere downstairs. Twig had caught a glimpse of him in the bathroom combing his hair. She was as far away as she could get, in her room with the door closed, doing her homework even though it was Friday night.

It was so quiet that her pencil sounded loud on the paper. She kept glancing over at the clock radio. 7:01. 7:03. She lost track of her math problem and had to start over.

The house held its breath.

At 7:06 a car honked outside. Two light honks, just

the way her father always did it when he picked her up at Annie's.

What if he came in? she thought suddenly. What if he walked right up the stairs to her room? What would she do?

But then she heard a door slam downstairs. The car hummed away into the distance. He was gone.

Twig breathed again. For a few minutes, while her heart slowed its hip-hopping in her chest, she was grateful that all of them were gone and she was alone. She could go away inside a math problem and not think about anything else. That was the good thing about math. It was like a faraway land where everything went by the rules. All neat, squared off, precise. Sometimes Twig thought she loved math more than anything.

The tall old clock that used to belong to Grandma Rose ticked softly in the hallway. It was the only sound.

Twig put down her pencil. She felt surrounded by empty space. And all that quiet. It seeped inside, making her feel hollow right down to her bones. She was alone inside a box. All of them were. Her mother at the library. Grandma Ruthie in some cave somewhere. Her father at his new apartment. Maybe everyone in the world lived in separate lonely boxes.

That familiar ache started in her throat again. At this very moment her father and Nathan were trying to get out of their boxes. Why did it seem so hard?

In silent sock feet Twig padded downstairs.

"Charley?" Her voice sounded loud to her. "Where are you?"

She found him in the den, sprawled with all four feet sticking straight out on the couch. How long had he been sleeping on the furniture? Did her mother know? "No furniture!" she used to tell him with a glare whenever he tried it, and he would slink guiltily away.

He opened a wary eye, as if expecting Twig to do the same.

"Charley boy," she crooned, sitting on the floor next to him. Reaching up, she stroked his paw and then his broad neck with all its extra folds of skin and finally his ear, his soft warm ear. He relaxed, sighing with pleasure.

"You're the best dog in the world," she told him. "You know that?" A half-remembered fragment of a song came to her and she hummed. "There's nothing finer, in all of Carolina."

His tail thumped, urging her on. But Twig sat up straight. "Come on, Charley," she said, getting to her feet.

He raised his head, surprised, but didn't move.

Twig tried for her mother's glare. "No furniture!" she said in her most severe voice.

Reluctantly he stretched and jumped down.

Taking him by his worn collar, Twig led him to the stairs. "Come on up," she invited.

Charley seemed confused by all the sudden rule changes. They had spent years, since he was a puppy, convincing him that he was a downstairs dog. He sat wagging his tail agreeably, looking at the stairs as if they were an impossible mountain peak. It took some coaxing, but finally he decided that Twig was serious, and bounded up the stairs.

In her room he snuffled around for awhile, investigating everything on her floor, poking his nose into open bureau drawers. Then he did his circle walk and curled up on the pink rag rug next to her bed.

This was just where she had imagined him. The room felt different now, the space filled up.

Twig finished her math homework, listening to his breathing. Even though it was early, she put on her pajamas and climbed into bed. She read a chapter in her library book, then, suddenly sleepy, turned out the light. She lay staring at the ceiling, one hand trailing down to rest on Charley's side. In an instant, it seemed, she was asleep.

Some time later she opened her eyes to see head-lights crawling across the window shade. Someone was coming home. Later still, half-awake, she was puzzled by a low plunking sound. It kept repeating, monotonous, over and over. Of course. Nathan's guitar.

"He's getting a little better," she murmured to Charley.

He stirred, and her hand found his ear. His soft warm ear.

11

In the morning Twig awoke to a different sound: digging.

It was her mother. From her window she could see her, small in jeans and Nathan's outgrown red-checked wool shirt, in the far corner of the backyard. She had a shovel in her hands. All around her, what used to be grass had been hacked into brown clumps of mud.

Her mother rested for a moment, leaning on the shovel. Then she started in again, attacking the earth.

Another shovelful turned over, green square into brown. What was she doing? Had she really gone crazy?

Twig padded downstairs, Charley's nails click-clicking behind her. While she drank her orange juice, she watched out the window. Her mother kept digging, ponytail bouncing, barely pausing to rest. She seemed possessed by a furious energy, as if something pent up too long had suddenly burst.

This was getting scary. Was she going to dig up the whole backyard?

"Hey." A heavy hand fell on Twig's shoulder. "What's going on out there?"

Nathan, his hair in sticking-up clumps, his eyes sleepy, peered outside. "This is weird," he mumbled.

But suddenly it wasn't. Twig remembered something Grandma Ruthie had said, about Grandpa digging up the whole backyard when they moved into their new house.

"I think maybe she's making a garden," she said.

"I hope so," muttered Nathan, shaking his head. He seemed relieved, though. Yawning, he began prowling through the cupboard for his cereal.

Twig stood by the window, watching her mother's bent back, listening to Nathan's spoon clink against his bowl. She thought about last night. Should she ask Nathan about their father? What would she ask?

What she really wanted to know was that he was totally miserable—sad and lonely and sorry he had left. But what if he wasn't? What if he had a nice new life and didn't miss them at all?

She was afraid to find out.

"Dad asked about you," Nathan said suddenly. "He said to tell you he wants to see you."

Anger blazed up immediately inside her. "Well, I don't want to see him."

"I told him you're learning to cook. And I can do laundry. He could use us at his place. It's pretty bad."

"Bad?"

"Small, needs paint. Looks like a pigpen. The man never hung up anything in his life."

Good, Twig said to herself. The thought snuck in through a back door: He won't stay. He'll come back.

"You ought to see him," Nathan said, in a strangely insistent voice that didn't sound like his. She turned to find him staring at her. "Really, Twig."

She was going to say "Absolutely not," but just then her mother came in the back door. Her clothes were splashed with mud. Dirt streaked her face. Her hair was a tangle. But there was a pink flush on her cheeks and light in her eyes.

"Did you see?" she said, smiling. "I'm planting a garden."

She lifted her arms toward the ceiling, stretching.

"Oh, my. Digging is such a misery for the back."

"Want some help?" offered Nathan.

Now she was making wide circles with her arms, backward and forward like a windmill.

"No," she answered, shaking her head. "I think I need to do this myself." She splashed water on her face, took a drink at the sink, then was gone again.

A whirlwind, thought Twig. That was the way her mother used to be, busy, excited, doing so many things at once. She had a flash of long-ago memory.

She is perched on top of the big slide. Sun sifts through tall umbrellas of trees. Far below a tiny boy on a tiny red tricycle rides in circles, around and around. She feels afraid up so high, clutching tight to the painted sides. But there is her mother at the bottom with outstretched arms, smiling, chattering, making silly faces.

"You can do it! Come on, sweetie, come to Mama!"

She lets go. A whoosh of speed, a blur of silver, and she is swooped into her mother's arms. They spin around dizzily, hugging and dancing. "You did it! You did it!" until they topple over, laughing, into soft grass.

Her mother kept digging. After awhile Nathan finished eating and wandered upstairs, but Twig continued to watch. Where would it end? Would she really keep going until all the grass was mud? Could she?

At last the digging stopped. Looking out, Twig saw a neat dark square carved into the corner of the yard. Not the whole yard after all. But large. Almost as big, she thought, as her room.

"I think I may have gotten carried away." Her mother came in the door, hunched over like an old woman. She slumped over the table with a sigh. "Oh, my aching back."

"Can I get you anything?" Twig asked.

"A bath," breathed her mother.

Twig ran water in the tub, so hot it steamed, and dropped in the lavender-smelling bath crystals she always liked.

"Thanks." Her mother smiled at her briefly.

She soaked in the bathtub forever. Then, still bent over, wrapped in her old terry-cloth robe, she crept away to take a nap.

The house was still again. Maybe that was the end of the garden. Maybe it had just been another of her mother's strange moments.

But it was only the beginning. Over the next few days more things happened to that dark square of chopped-up dirt in the backyard.

One afternoon Twig came home from school to find her mother raking. She picked out rocks, broke up wet clumps, carefully smoothed out the soil until it looked like a flat brown blanket. Another day great bags of something lay next to the dirt. "Peat Moss" and "Organic Fertilizer," said the bags in large letters. Her mother mixed and sprinkled and raked some more.

A fence appeared. And a wheelbarrow. The backyard was beginning to resemble a farm.

Her mother looked exhausted. She soaked in lavender baths every night and went to bed early.

Finally one afternoon, while Twig was pouring milk for her snack, she looked out to see thin lines of white string cutting across the brown square. Next to one of them knelt her mother, head close to the earth. She was dropping in seeds.

On the kitchen counter sat the box they had come in. Twig looked inside. It was empty except for a small slip of paper, like a sheet torn from a grocery pad. On it, in Grandma Ruthie's writing, was scrawled, "When you garden, you put your troubles into the ground."

12

One minute the trees were lacy skeletons.

The next they wore leaves of the softest, youngest green. Twig never saw it happen. Every year she tried, but while she slept or looked away just for a moment, buds burst into leaves.

Flowers too. Crocuses poked up their heads shyly in the grass. Forsythia shouted. Daffodils waved in a bright yellow line along the driveway.

Twig and her mother had planted those daffodils together the year they moved into the house, when she was five.

It is a sunny day in early fall. They work together as a team, she and Mommy. First Mommy kneels to dig a hole, like a deep dark pocket in the ground. Twig drops in the bulb, careful to keep its pointy side up. Then both of them cover it with handfuls of moist black soil.

The sun feels warm in her hair. Fall leaves drift lazily down, spattering the lawn with yellow handprints. The day smells like damp earth and dry leaves. Twig holds a daf-

fodil bulb in her hand, round and papery brown-white like an onion, and wonders how it can possibly turn into a flower.

"Where does the flower come from?" she asks later.

Her mother doesn't answer right away. She shakes her head, smiling, as they wash up at the kitchen sink, Twig on a step stool, scrubbing her hands with a brush. "It's a mystery," she says finally, fingers ruffling Twig's hair, "how things grow—flowers or puppies or kids. Truly an amazement."

And it was. The following spring the daffodils popped up: first dark, slender leaves, then an amazing explosion of yellow, like cheery smiling faces. She and Mommy had done that, Twig thought proudly. Together.

Remembering, Twig had a longing to be outside now working next to her mother. She could help. She could drop in the seeds or cover them up. Or just hand her things. But something held her back. It was true that her mother seemed different these past few days, filled with new energy, her eyes bright with a fierce determination. Dirt smudged her face and made circles on the knees of her jeans, like Nathan's when he used to build dirt towns. Like him, she fell into bed unconscious each night after her bath. Still, she wasn't herself. She was somewhere else, alone.

So Twig kept watching from her bedroom window. Spying, really.

More strings appeared, marking off more rows. It reminded Twig of a giant math problem. She could just hear Mr. Girardi. "If Farmer Jones plants seven rows of corn, four rows of peas, two rows of beans, and one row of carrots, what fraction of his garden is corn?"

More seed packets turned up on the kitchen table. Her mother had been to the garden center again. She planted cucumbers and two kinds of squash.

Something nudged at Twig's memory. She thought of Grandma Ruthie sitting at that same table, talking about Grandpa's long-ago garden. Those were all the things he had planted. Her mother was making a garden just like his.

A neat row of poles sprung up, like a backbone down the middle of the garden. Something was going to grow on them. Of course: the sugar snap peas.

Then came the books, a tall stack on the kitchen counter. *Building Your Compost Pile* was the title on top.

A few more days, and a round wire bin took shape next to the garden. And suddenly her mother was separating the garbage, taking out vegetable peelings and lettuce leaves, eggshells and coffee grounds. Mixing and stirring and tossing in that bin as if she were making a giant salad.

Finally there was a pause.

The garden waited, as square and tidy as a patch on a quilt. Her mother rested, while mists of spring rain turned the grass bottle-green and the earth black.

The rain continued for three days, then stopped. It was just before dinner. Looking out her window, Twig saw the backyard all bright and fresh-washed. Sun glinted in the wet grass. Along its edges, uncurling ferns stretched for the sky. The little tree in the back corner, given to their mother one Mother's Day, was covered with new puffs of pink. And the garden—something looked different, blurry, in the dark square of garden.

Her mother was outside, kneeling next to her strings, looking. A moment later she came hurrying into the house.

"Nathan! Twig! Come see what's happened!"

They both popped out of their rooms. Nathan rolled his eyes at Twig as they followed their mother outside.

At first Twig didn't see anything at all. Then, in the row marked "Sugar Snap Peas," she made out the tiniest curled leaf poking up from the ground. And another. And a bigger one in the "Bush Beans" row.

"Hey," exclaimed Nathan in a low surprised voice.

Twig looked where he was looking.

A line of green fuzz, feathery fine, had sprung out of the earth. It marched in a nearly straight line beneath its string down the center of the garden.

"It's like fur," marveled Twig.

"Or green hair," added Nathan. "Weird."

Their mother's face wore a broad grin, like the proud parent of a newborn baby.

"It's carrots," she said.

13

Twig was walking up the driveway when she saw it.

She was coming home from school, carrying her books and her Ancient Egypt project and the mail she had just taken from the mailbox. She put everything down to look.

It was tiny and reddish brown and sat absolutely still, nearly invisible next to the stone wall. She thought at first it was a mouse, but she couldn't see a tail. Then she noticed the long ears pressed flat against its head. It was a baby rabbit.

She knelt down. The rabbit didn't move or even twitch.

"Hey, bunny," she whispered.

How had it gotten there? Had it fallen out of its nest? But rabbits lived in holes in the ground, she thought. Had it wandered away from its mother? It must be very young, too young to leave its mother. What if the neighbors' mean cat found it? Or an owl or a hawk looking down from the sky?

Twig didn't know what to do. She needed to ask someone. But her mother's car was gone. Probably she was at the library or the garden center. Nathan was at track practice, naturally.

"Stay right there," she told the rabbit. It would be safe next to the wall, as long as that nasty cat didn't come along. She looked around. No sign of a lurking gray shadow. Good.

Twig unlocked the back door and went right to the phone. Who should she call? Annie wasn't home. She had her violin lesson today. Their science teacher would be good to ask. But she'd seen him leaving school when she got on the bus. The nature center— that was it. She looked up the number and dialed. It rang and rang, but no one answered. Twig glanced at the clock. 4:10. The nature center closed at four o'clock.

She was going to have to do this on her own. A box. That was what she needed. She ran down to the basement and grabbed an empty carton, then hurried back outside.

The baby rabbit was exactly where she had left it. It hadn't moved an inch. Probably that was what its mother had told it: In case of trouble, stay quiet and no one will notice you.

Where was its mother anyway? Why didn't she come and rescue her baby? Didn't she care? Suddenly Twig was very angry at the mother rabbit.

It was up to her. Carefully she set down the box on its side near the baby.

"Come on, bunny," she crooned softly.

Maybe it would hop right in. But it didn't. Twig knelt down so that the rabbit was between her and the box. Very slowly she moved closer, hoping it would back into the box.

Still it sat motionless. Not a blink. Not a quiver. It was as if it were in some kind of trance.

It was so small and helpless. Twig reached out her hands.

Suddenly the rabbit jumped. Startled, Twig caught it against the stone wall. She didn't know who was more surprised, she or the rabbit. She could feel its fear, the leap of its heart through soft fur. And something else way inside: its bones. It trembled against her fingers, then was still again. Was it dead? Could she have frightened it to death?

Quickly she set it down inside the box. Oh please, don't let it be dead.

The rabbit crouched in a corner. Its eyes were open. It seemed to be breathing. Yes, it was alive.

Now what?

"It's all right," she murmured, trying to calm it and herself. "I'm going to take care of you."

Food. She should give it something to eat. Babies ate all the time. The rabbits that visited their yard always seemed to be nibbling on grass. Twig carried the box to the lawn. She pulled up handfuls of grass and piled it in a corner.

"Go ahead, little bunny," she whispered. "Eat."

But the rabbit stayed huddled right where it was. Maybe it was too scared to eat. Or maybe grass wasn't the right food. Babies mostly needed milk.

Twig remembered a book she had once read where someone found a baby animal—a squirrel? a raccoon?—and fed it milk from a medicine dropper. How exactly did that work? Was it regular milk or some special kind? Was it mixed with something else? She couldn't remember. She couldn't try to feed this baby without knowing just how to do it.

Maybe she should leave the rabbit alone for a few minutes. If she wasn't watching, it might eat the grass.

But what if it was cold? She couldn't be sure, but she thought she saw it trembling again. Twig left the box next to the back door and ran up to her room. In her bottom drawer she found her too-small T-shirt with the chipmunk and rabbit faces on it from the nature center. Perfect. She ran downstairs and wadded up the shirt to fill the bottom of the box.

There. That made a cozy rabbit's nest.

"What have you got there?"

Twig looked up into Nathan's face, his eyebrows knit together quizzically like two V's. Why did he keep looking like their father? Was it an accident, or did he know he used the exact same expressions?

"I found it in the driveway," she explained.

He knelt down next to her, peering into the box. "Wow," he breathed. "Isn't it amazing that something so small can be put together so perfectly?"

It was just what she was thinking. For a moment they both stared silently. The rabbit twitched its nose. Twig and Nathan let out their breath at the same time. Suddenly Twig felt oddly peaceful and happy. It was nice to be sharing this with someone, not to be alone.

"What are you going to do with it?" asked Nathan finally.

"I don't know," said Twig.

She told him about finding the rabbit and trying to call someone and trying to feed it. "It won't eat," she said. "Maybe grass is the wrong thing. Maybe it needs milk. I don't know what to do."

Nathan looked thoughtful. "I saw a rabbit, a big one, a couple of times over by the lilac bushes. You know, where all that overgrown stuff is near the driveway? That could be where the nest is. Maybe if you put it back there, the mother would come and find it."

No, thought Twig. She didn't want to do that. What she wanted to do was feed the baby rabbit herself with a medicine dropper, like in the book. She would save its life. Then the rabbit would be hers and would need her and she wouldn't be alone.

"But what if that's not where the nest is?" she argued. "And the Atwoods' cat comes and finds it instead? I think we should keep it. I'll take care of it." She had a sudden thought. "We can go to the library and get a book on how to feed it and everything. That's it. When Mom comes home, she can take me. Or you could ride over on your bike."

Nathan was shaking his head while she was talking.

"It needs its mother, Twig," he said quietly.

A tear welled up unexpectedly in her eye. Of course. Everyone needed a mother. But sometimes mothers left you alone. Then what were you supposed to do?

Nathan stood up. "I need a drink," he said.

He went inside, banging the storm door shut. That door would be on all summer, since no one but her father knew how to change to the screen door.

Twig gazed down at the rabbit, its tiny whiskers, its perfect pinkish ears, so thin you could almost see through them. It still hadn't budged from its corner, but she thought it didn't seem quite so scared. It was getting used to her. She could take care of it, she knew she could.

Oh, but what if she couldn't? What if it never would eat? What if the baby rabbit died, pining for its mother?

Pining for its mother. Her throat closed up so she couldn't swallow. There was no doubt what she had to do. It wasn't a choice.

Twig picked up the box, and balancing it carefully so as not to frighten the baby any more, she carried it over to the lilac bushes. Nathan was right. The tangle of leaves and branches and snaky-looking roots could easily hide a rabbit's nest. Pushing underneath as far as she could, so no cats or watching hawks could see, she gently set down the box.

"It's okay, bunny," she reassured it.

Very slowly she tipped the box on its side, so the rabbit would be able to hop out. She heard scrabbling of feet on cardboard. "It's all right, sweetie," she said softly. "I'm still here." Then, silence.

She had to leave so whatever was going to happen could happen.

"'Bye, little bunny," she whispered, and stood up.

Twig checked all around for rabbit enemies. She walked to the front of the house, then all the way around back just to be sure. She stood by the back door, listening. Finally she went inside. Nathan had gone upstairs. Through the ceiling she could hear the faint over-and-over throb of his guitar.

She poured herself a drink of juice in her rabbit mug. Sitting down at the kitchen table, Twig took out her English homework. Fifteen minutes, she told herself. She would wait fifteen minutes before she went back outside. Maybe twenty. A half hour would be even better.

Fourteen minutes later, walking toward the lilac bushes, she caught sight of something in the grass. Her first thought was the cat next door.

But no. It was a rabbit: a big one.

It sat perfectly still, like a painting of a rabbit, long brown ears up, nose twitching. Then, seeing her, it hopped away, its white tail bobbing. Could this be the mother?

Twig knelt down to look under the bushes. The box was there, just where she'd left it. Heart pounding, she slid it toward her. It was empty.

So it must have happened the way Nathan had said. This was where the baby rabbit lived. Somewhere under the ground, it was curled up now in a warm cozy nest with its brothers and sisters, probably telling them all about its adventure. Its mother had gone out, but she would be right back and she would take good care of it.

Twig felt herself filling up with hope. Most likely everything was going to be all right.

She stood up, dumping the grass from the box. Then, as an afterthought, she bent to arrange it in a pile, in case the baby rabbit would like some as a snack.

"Hey, little bunny," she called softly into the bushes. "Grow up good."

14

More seeds came in the mail from Grandma Ruthie.

This time they were flowers: marigolds and zinnias and a blue one, the color of sky, called morning glory.

"All the flowers your grandpa used to grow," sighed Twig's mother.

Twig had a picture in her head of Grandpa in his garden, wearing a straw farmer's hat and surrounded by flowers. The garden was like a jungle, all colors of flowers and leaves and climbing vines, and Grandpa smiled out of the middle of it, crinkly skin, twinkly bright blue eyes. Had she seen that picture in some old photo album? Or was she really remembering Grandpa, who had died when she was three?

And here was another mystery. When Grandpa was alive, he and Grandma Ruthie lived in the same little house in the same little town for years and years. But after Grandpa died, Grandma Ruthie sold the house and started traveling, and she hadn't sat still a minute since. Why was that?

"There's something for you."

Her mother handed Twig a packet of seeds. "Mammoth Sunflowers," the label read. Attached to it was a note. "Twig: 'To dig and delve in nice clean dirt can do a mortal little hurt.' Have fun! Love, Grandma."

"What does that mean?" Twig asked, handing it to her mother.

"Oh, my." A smile crinkled her eyes. "I'd almost forgotten. That old saying was carved on a stone in your grandpa's garden."

" 'Grows six to nine feet tall,' " Twig read out loud from the seed packet. "Wow! They're not kidding about mammoth."

"Sunflowers are fun," her mother said. "Easy too. And you can save the seeds to feed the birds in winter."

Twig took a deep breath, looking up at her mother. "Will you help me plant them?"

"Of course."

They crouched side by side, their faces close to the earth. Her mother was planting zinnias. Twig was doing the sunflowers.

First you made a shallow trench with the tip of the trowel, careful to keep a straight line. That was what the strings were for: to guide you. Then you dropped in a seed. The sunflower seeds were huge compared to the zinnia seeds, which you could barely see. And the morning glories. You covered up the seed with half an inch of dirt and pressed it down firmly. Then, about six inches farther down the row, you dropped in the next seed.

They didn't talk much. They were too busy. Dig, plant, cover up. Dig, plant, cover up. There was a rhythm to the work and a focus on just this little patch of earth and nothing else that was soothing. The sun beat warm on Twig's back. Birds twittered. A bee droned around a flowering bush. The rest of the world seemed to recede into the distance.

Glancing over, Twig noticed that her mother looked peaceful too. She blew back a lock of hair, not even realizing she was doing it. She looked almost like a child. A child in her father's garden.

Twig dropped in the next seed and covered it with dirt. Like a blanket, she thought. She was keeping it warm so it could grow. She had never really looked at dirt before. Not so much of it. Not up close like this. It was gray and powdery on top, since it hadn't rained for a few days. But when she dug down with the trowel, it became dark and rich-looking, soil in which plants couldn't help but grow. She supposed it was all those bags of planting stuff her mother had mixed in.

An earthworm wriggled next to Twig's trowel.

Another surprising thing was how many tiny creatures lived here, all hidden away until you dug into the dirt. Besides earthworms, there were dark little beetles that scuttled away, hiding from the light, when they were disturbed. And an odd-looking silvery insect with so many legs that it seemed to roll instead of walk. That one was a centipede, she thought. Could it really have a hundred legs? And a green bug so small that climbing out of Twig's trench must feel to it like scaling a mountain.

Where was the green bug going? Was it looking for food? Or was it scaling mountains and crossing deserts on its way to somewhere else? Did it have a plan, or was it just wandering around? It looked to her as if it knew where it was going. But insects couldn't think. Or could they? What if a whole different miniature world existed here in the dirt, and things were happening just like they did in the human world?

Maybe the green bug had just run away from home. Or was on its way to visit its cousin on the far side of the garden. Or had set out on a quest to find the tastiest leaves in all the land. Twig watched as it finally reached the summit of her trench, then struck out toward the carrot row. That was miles away for the green bug. Did it know how dangerous this journey could be? A bigger bug might eat it. Or a bird. Or

Twig might step on it by mistake. It might never return home. Would its family wonder what had happened to it? Would they be sad?

Twig had the power to change that green bug's life. If she felt mean, she could squash it. Or capture it in a jar. Or she could put a finger down and force it to change direction, so it never would reach the carrot row. The thought made her feel odd. It was scary to have that much power, just because you were a bigger creature.

Maybe she would write a story about the green bug for English. What would happen if it looked up and saw her, a huge menacing shadow blocking out the sun? Or just her hand holding the sharp trowel? Would the green bug think its land had been invaded by a creature from another planet? "Green Bug Meets the Alien"—that's what she would call it. It would be kind of a science fiction story. The green bug was a messenger, like Paul Revere. Right now it was on its way to warn all the other bugs in the kingdom of this giant invader with its terrible sword. "The War of the Garden"—maybe that was a better title.

"Twig," her mother whispered, "look at this."

She was staring down at something near her right sneaker. Twig couldn't make out what it was. She stood up.

Her mother remained completely still. "Move slowly," she warned.

Twig knelt down next to her. Right by the dusty toe of her sneaker was a small brown toad. It was precisely the color of dirt, bumpy and lumpy-looking. It didn't move either. But it didn't seem afraid. It was as if the toad knew no one could see it in its perfect camouflage.

Something pulsed in its throat—its heart beating? Twig thought it seemed even more fragile than the green bug. Just a puff of skin over a beating heart.

"Isn't nature astonishing?" her mother murmured.

Twig had a sudden urge to touch it, to see what that skin felt like.

She reached out a finger, but her mother caught her hand.

"Don't scare it away," she said softly. "A toad is good luck in the garden, your grandpa always said. Besides, it eats insects."

Watch out, green bug, thought Twig.

Her mother didn't move her hand. It was warm on hers. The toad didn't move either.

"It's going to stay," Twig whispered.

They both smiled.

15

Twig couldn't stop looking at one photograph.

It was on her mother's bureau. She didn't know why it was still there. The room was rearranged now, a new quilt on the bed, a comfortable reading chair dragged in from the den, spilling over with books and papers. But every time Twig passed it, she felt herself drawn to look again. The photograph had been taken on her mother and father's wedding day.

After the ceremony, outside the church, people are throwing rice at the bride and groom. You can see them at both sides of the picture, smiling wide exuberant smiles. A lady in a straw hat, her mouth open, arm drawn back taking aim. A little girl in a pink polka-dot dress. Her father's cousin Sam, his hand actually reaching into her father's jacket pocket. But her mother and father aren't looking at them. They are gazing straight at each other, as if they can't see anything else. As if nothing else in the world exists.

They had loved each other then. How could that

change? Was it possible for it to just stop one day? What had gone wrong?

She needed to know. Love was supposed to go on forever.

Twig searched for clues. She looked in the photo albums that were piled on a shelf in the den, documenting just about every minute of Nathan's life when he was a baby, slightly fewer of hers, then dwindling down gradually as they grew older to mostly holidays and vacation trips. Her mother and father hardly appeared during the baby years, and almost never together. There was Mom holding Nathan on a merry-go-round horse. Dad with toothless Twig on his lap. Dad and Nathan feeding the elephants at the zoo. Mom, Nathan, and Twig, looking terrified, talking to Santa Claus. But then she came across a photo marked, in her mother's neat handwriting, "Sixth Anniversary."

Her parents sit on a bench, maybe outside a restaurant, her father's arm loosely draped over her mother's shoulder. Her hand, holding a pair of sunglasses, rests on his knee. It seems to be summer. Of course, they were married in July. Her mother's hair is shorter than Twig ever remembers it. Everything is green around them, and sunny, and that is how their faces seem: bright, young, carefree. They are looking at the camera, not at each other, not ex-

actly smiling. But both of their mouths have the tiniest up-ward curve.

They had been happy that day, she was sure of it.

Another album. She and Nathan grew older. She rode a red tricycle. He proudly climbed the steps of the school bus for the first day of school. By this time her father was the official family photographer, so he was rarely seen in pictures. It was Mom who steadied Nathan as he rode his two-wheeler for the first time, Mom who lifted Twig onto a slide shaped like a giraffe. But every now and then there was a family photo of the four of them, taken by someone else. Nathan and Twig—still round-faced, he looking squirmy, she smiling brightly—were always between their parents in these pictures. Her mother and father had an arm around them, looked at them, not at each other.

Twig took down more dusty albums. She saw herself as a ballet dancer, Halloween princess, pirate in the second-grade play. She saw trips to the ocean and Grandma Rose's cabin on the lake. She saw a lot of Christmas trees. This was like flipping through her life.

Finally she came to the last photo album. This one was only half full. No one had put pictures in it for a long time. The most recent ones were from last summer, from their vacation in Maine. Fishing boats tied up at a pier. The restaurant where they ate lobsters outside on picnic tables. The island they sailed to, in seas so rough that everyone but her mother got seasick. Her father's face had actually turned green that day, she remembered.

They stand on a cliff overlooking the ocean, Twig and her mother and father. After all the rough water, the day has suddenly cleared and both sky and sea are so perfectly blue, you can hardly believe they are real. The wind blows Twig's hair across her face. She has grown nearly as tall as her tiny mother, she notices. She and her mother lean toward each other, their shoulders just barely touching. Her father stands slightly apart from them, his back very straight, arms crossed. His face still looks a little green.

Her father seemed alone in that picture, Twig thought. She and her mother were together, and he wasn't quite with them.

Had it already started then, whatever it was that had divided her parents? Had things been different between them during that vacation? Or was it just that her father was having a bad day, feeling seasick and all?

She searched her memory. There must have been a moment when everything changed. She should have seen it. She should have known. But hard as Twig tried, she couldn't remember. It was like looking through fog. The only clues she had were the pictures, flat and cold, tiny fragments of the past caught on paper.

Her mother and father on their wedding day. Her mother and father and Twig, perched on a cliff.

16

Nathan had combed his hair again.

"Where are you going?" Twig asked him.

He flashed her a look. "How do you know I'm going somewhere?"

She pointed at her own hair.

"Oh. Dad's taking me out for a burger and a baseball game." He was also wearing a plaid shirt she'd never seen before, one with a collar and buttons. He hesitated, then asked, "Want to come?"

"Of course not." There it came again, that sudden squirt of anger. She scowled at Nathan.

"I know, I know." He sighed loudly. "You think I shouldn't go either. Well, I am. Whatever has happened or is going to happen in this family, I still want Dad in my life."

Twig stared at him, surprised. He didn't usually sound this way, so sure about things.

"Hey, I know you're angry," he went on, picking up steam. "I am too. We all are. But you know what your problem is? I figured it out. You're stuck. You don't want to admit that anything has changed. If you don't see Dad, you can keep pretending it is all the way it used to be. Well, it's not. And it never will be again."

"I know that," protested Twig.

"You do but you don't." Nathan's voice got softer. "The thing is we have to move on, figure out some new kind of life. Because everything has changed, and it's not going to change back. Dad has changed. He has a beard now."

A beard? Her father? She couldn't imagine it. He had never had one before, not even in the photographs of when he was young.

"Reddish," said Nathan. "Kind of curly. Looks good."

Twig wondered about all the other things Nathan had said. Were they true? She didn't think so, but her thoughts were too jumbled to sort out.

Something flashed by the front window. Twig had a

fleeting glimpse of a man. Tall, blue sweater. Reddish beard. The doorbell rang, two short beeps like a car horn.

"He's early," Nathan said.

Oh, my. Twig's breath caught sharply. She hadn't recognized him. Her own father. He looked like a stranger.

Without her telling them to, her feet were moving.

"Hey." Nathan reached out a hand. "At least say hello."

But Twig was already at the back door. She could hear her father's voice, a distant rumble somewhere behind, as she started to run.

"Pearl," she thought she heard. Was he calling her, or was it just the wind in her ears?

She was fleeing, she said to herself. It was one of the last week's vocabulary words. "Fleeing the scene of the crime" had been the example. Running felt good. She stretched her legs and kept going, as if she were in a race. Trees flew by, streaming green. Cars in driveways, a yapping white dog on a chain, the lilac bushes at the corner in a burst of perfume. Her legs were light under her, smooth as silver. She wasn't tired. She could run forever.

A face floated in space above her head: reddish beard, kind of curly. A face she knew so well, yet didn't know. It was scary. How dare he go and grow a beard?

They sit across from each other on the living room rug, his long legs crossed, the coffee table between them. On it is the checkerboard, set up for their regular Saturday morning game. She is red and he is black, as always, and she is winning, which is rare. Her father doesn't believe in losing on purpose. In front of Twig is a pile of his black checkers that she has captured. It is a tall pile. She has him down to his last king.

Her father is pondering his next move. His hand rests on his king. He starts to move, then thinks better of it, scratching his head.

Twig clicks her pile of checkers impatiently. She has him surrounded. She can't wait for him to make his move so she can win.

"Go ahead," she urges, unable to stand it another minute.

He frowns at her.

Then suddenly he is running his hands through his hair, pulling at it until it all stands up wildly on end, like a mad scientist. "What am I going to do?" he wails loudly, pretending to cry. "How can I escape?"

"You can't," says Twig, smiling.

"You're right," agrees her father. "I give up."

He makes his move. She takes his king.

They shake hands solemnly, as they always do at the end of a game.

"Nice going," says her father.

Looking at his silly, curly, sticking-on-end hair, she laughs.

Twig ran faster. Past the pond, with its four white ducks quietly paddling. Past the playground. Out of the corner of her eye, she saw the giraffe slide. After awhile she noticed that she was crying, but she didn't slow down.

She kept on running. Away.

17

Eventually she had to stop.

Her chest felt tight and hot. She had a nagging stitch in her side. Twig looked up to find herself on Annie's street. Her knees felt suddenly weak as she picked her way across the toy-strewn lawn to Annie's back door.

Her mother opened it, a bowl of salad in her hands. Behind her, something boiled on the stove, sending up clouds of steam. Annie's three-year-old brother, Brandon, was crawling around on the floor. Seeing Twig, he sat up and began to bark.

"Don't mind him." Annie's mother smiled. "He's a dog right now." She hugged Twig, salad and all. "I'm so glad to see you. Come in."

Twig hesitated. "I'm sorry. I didn't know it was dinnertime."

"Don't be silly. There's always plenty of casserole. Just call your mom and tell her you're staying for supper."

Brandon seemed to want her to stay. He wagged his rear end and licked her ankle.

"Well," said Twig, "okay. Thanks."

"Annie!" called her mother. "Come see who's here. And set another place at the table."

Dinner at Annie's house was always unusual. First they had to get Brandon to change himself back into a boy.

"Come on, fruitcake," Annie urged. "Show Twig how you do it."

"You take two of these," Brandon explained, swallowing invisible pills. "And—poof—you're a dog. Want to try it?" He lay down under the kitchen table.

"No," laughed Annie. "Not those pills, the other ones."

"Oh," he said. His eyes, looking up at them, were

serious under a mop of light doggy-looking hair. "Okay. You take two of these purple ones." He swallowed again. "And—poof—you're not a dog any-more." And he climbed into his chair.

Then they had to get Annie's other brother, Kevin, and her father to the table. Her mother called and called. Finally they came in, baseball caps on both heads, mitts on their hands, their moon-shaped faces looking exactly alike.

They hung their mitts on their chairs.

"What's wrong with this picture?" asked Annie's mother, spoon poised to serve the casserole.

"Hats at the table?" said her father.

"Hats at the table," said her mother.

"But, Mom," protested Kevin, "we're ballplayers. It's our uniform. We have to wear them."

"That's right," added Annie's father. "The hats are the secrets of our power. If we take them off, we strike out."

Annie's mother stared at him. She looked like a statue: Woman Holding a Spoon.

Annie's father stared back: Man Wearing a Too-Small Baseball Cap.

"Hmmm," he said. "On the other hand, maybe chicken casserole is the secret of our power."

Removing both hats, he hung them on the chairs.

That was the way the entire dinner went. Annie's

mother and father argued over everything: baseball teams, the spices in the chicken casserole, who was supposed to have called the repairman about the broken washing machine, the diet he was always on.

And the chocolate-chip cookies.

"I'm sorry there aren't more," Annie's mother said, setting down a small plate in front of Twig. "I just baked them yesterday. There were plenty in the cookie jar at lunchtime. There were plenty while I was making the casserole. But sometime before dinner, a cookie thief must have crept into the house and made off with a huge handful."

She stared pointedly at Annie's father.

"Me?" he said. "I'm a ballplayer. I'm in training. I'm in shape."

"You are also a chocolate-chip cookie fanatic."

"This may be. But I am restrained about it. I have willpower."

"Unless you happen to see one or smell one. Or hear a rumor of the existence of one."

Brandon was tugging at his mother's sleeve. She leaned over, and he whispered loudly in her ear. "Pongo did it."

"Pongo?"

Brandon nodded solemnly.

"That's his name when he's a dog," said Annie, rolling her eyes at Twig.

"And why would Pongo take so many cookies?"

"They're not cookies," he whispered, looking at the floor. "They're dog biscuits."

A smile pricked at the corners of Annie's mother's mouth. She looked across the table at Annie's father. All at once they both burst out laughing.

"Falsely accused once again," he said, reaching for a cookie.

"Well, you wish you'd done it. In your heart you know you do."

Looking satisfied that she'd had the last word, she snatched the chocolate-chip cookie out of his hand, and bit into it.

Twig walked home through the pale green twilight, thinking about Annie's parents. All that arguing they always did made her nervous. She wasn't used to it. Everything was so noisy at Annie's house. Interesting to watch, kind of like a movie, but unsettling.

Arguing wasn't good, was it? Wasn't it a sign of trouble? But her parents had never argued. No bickering. No raised voices. She couldn't remember a single fight. And now they were separated, getting a divorce. There was a clue here somewhere.

Actually, she thought, remembering the dinner, something about all that arguing was nice. It wasn't angry. It was friendly. Almost like a game. Like Ping-Pong. One of them served and the other hit it back, and they kept going—back and forth, back and forth—until they missed or got tired of it. And all the time the game went on, something was happening between them. They paid attention to each other. They were connected.

Twig felt in her pocket. The recipe that Annie's mother had given her was still there. Tomorrow after school she was going to try making those chocolate-chip cookies. And she'd save a few for Pongo.

18

Things were starting to happen in the garden.

Twig's sunflowers pushed up out of the dirt and immediately, it seemed, began reaching for the sun. They must grow an inch a day, she thought in amazement.

The other flower plants were tiny in comparison. But they too lifted their baby leaves bravely, forming new rows next to the peas and bush beans and carrots. Along the fence morning glory shoots popped up, then sprouted little tendrils that wound around the wire, vines-to-be that would some day support sky-blue flowers.

The sugar snap peas had vines now too, Twig saw. Frail curling green fingers waved around, found the strings, and began to climb up her mother's pole trellis.

"It works!" Her mother beamed. "I thought I remembered how your grandpa used to do it, but I wasn't sure."

Just one still-brown space remained at the back of the garden.

Before Twig had a chance to ask about it, her mother came home from the garden center with a tray of spindly droopy little plants.

"Smell," she invited, waving them under Twig's nose. "Do you know what these are?"

The smell was familiar, teasing at the edge of her memory. Twig shook her head.

"Tomatoes!" said her mother triumphantly. "You can't have a real garden without them. And this is tomato-planting time. Grandpa always used to say, 'Peas by Saint Patrick's Day, tomatoes by Memorial Day.'"

Of course. That's what had been missing.

"They don't look like much now, I admit. But just

wait a few weeks. By August we'll be having a tomato feast. Oh, I can't wait! Biting into a ripe tomato is like tasting summer." She looked young, excited, the way she used to. Something about planting things seemed to do that to her.

"And can we wash them off with the hose and eat them right in the garden?" Twig asked.

"Absolutely," said her mother.

They planted the tomatoes together, Twig digging the holes while her mother fussed over each one with compost and fertilizer before gently tucking it into the ground.

Like putting a baby to bed, Twig thought.

"Of course I bought too many," her mother lamented cheerfully as they crowded in the last one. "I tried to restrain myself, but it's so hard. Grandpa always had a million tomatoes. They'd be piled up in bowls and on windowsills, and Grandma Ruthie would be cooking up big batches of spaghetti sauce and he'd give them away to half the neighborhood besides."

She straightened up, giving the last tomato plant a pat on the head. "There you go." Looking around, she frowned. "Uh-oh, it's starting."

"What's starting?"

"The weed invasion."

Following her mother's gaze, Twig saw what she meant. Those fat leaves among the slim feathery ones were not carrots.

"What do you do about that?"

"I show them no mercy. Want to help?"

Weeding was no fun. Soon Twig's jeans had wet brown knees. She was hot and dirty and her back ached from bending over, and some kind of bug kept buzzing in her ear. When she slapped at it, dirt spread to her shirt. And it wasn't just a few weeds, they were everywhere. Where had they come from so suddenly? And why did there seem to be more weeds than the things they'd planted on purpose?

But after awhile that same peaceful feeling began creeping over her. All she saw was brown earth and green growing things. All she felt was warm sun. It was satisfying to yank out the bad guys, those weed invaders, so the good guys would have room to grow, to make the rows neat and tidy. It was hard work, but it felt good seeing what you had done. Bringing order to just this little piece of ground.

The other thing was her mother. All the time they were weeding, she was talking. She hadn't talked so much in months. It was as if some stopper inside had broken and words came spilling out like water.

"There must be a better way," she muttered, frowning, as she too swatted at bugs. "Actually there is. I remember now. Grandpa used to spread a special kind of hay between the rows to keep down weeds. I'll get a couple of bales tomorrow. Maybe Nathan can help me carry it."

"That sounds good," said Twig, relieved.

"One more thing." Her mother pointed at the carrot row. "Do you notice how close together those plants are? They need thinning. You have to pull out some so the others will have room to grow. Otherwise they'll bump into each other. Grandpa always hated thinning. He said it was like murdering your children. You know what he did once? He couldn't bear to throw away the thinnings, so he planted them in the front yard between all Grandma Ruthie's zinnias and marigolds and petunias."

"Did they grow?"

"They certainly did. They looked a little odd and Grandma Ruthie didn't like it much, but that year Grandpa picked carrots from the front yard all the way till Thanksgiving."

Her mother laughed. The sound startled Twig. When was the last time she had heard her mother laugh?

"I've been thinking a lot about your grandpa lately," she went on, bent over again. "Because of the garden, I suppose. He was a tenderhearted man. Big, strong. Those eyes could burn a hole in you if you did something wrong. But gentle. I really miss him. Do you remember him, Twig?"

Somewhere fuzzily in the back of her mind, she thought she did.

Blue smiling eyes. Large rough hands. She bounces up and down on dark blue knees. "Row, row, row your boat," they sing together, "gently down the stream. Merrily, merrily, merrily, merrily. Life is but a—" Here he pauses, and she does too, holding her breath in delicious anticipation. And then: "peanut-butter sandwich!" he finishes. Or something just as silly, like "school bus" or "double-fudge ice-cream cone." She laughs and laughs as his arms go around her, strong yet careful, in a big bear hug.

"I think so. We played a game. 'Row, Row, Row Your Boat.'"

"That's right, you did." Her mother smiled. "It's strange, but when Grandpa died, Grandma Ruthie couldn't stay in that house anymore. It hurt too much, she said. Nearly thirty years in one place, happy with her flowers and her cooking and working part-time at the library as a storyteller, and then she just completely changed her life. Sold the house and all the furniture, moved to a tiny apartment, and started taking trips. And she hasn't sat still for a minute since."

Her mother's voice trailed off, as if she were still trying to puzzle it out.

Carefully Twig pulled a weed from between two carrot plants, then patted the soil until it was smooth.

"Why?" she asked in the sudden silence.

Her mother looked over at her. "I think she started out trying to forget. She was so terribly sad after Grandpa died. But then after awhile, she discovered that she really loved traveling. The adventure, the independence—" Abruptly she stopped. "But that wasn't what you were asking, was it?"

Twig shook her head.

Her mother closed her eyes, shivering as if a cold wind had come up. There was no wind. For a long time she said nothing.

Then, quietly, "Do you see my two rows of zinnias?"

Twig looked. Her mother must have laid out the strings crookedly. At the beginning of the rows, the little plants were evenly spaced. But as they went along, they got farther and farther apart.

Her mother spoke slowly, carefully. "Your father and I started out close and happy. We thought we wanted the same things. We both certainly wanted you and Nathan. But somewhere along the way, so slowly that we didn't notice it happening, we began drifting apart. Like those two flower rows."

She reached out a finger and touched one of the baby plants gently.

"Maybe it was our jobs. We both tend to get so absorbed in our work. Maybe it was just us. I can't explain it or even understand it myself. For a long time we pretended it wasn't happening. You see, I wanted desperately for Dad and me to be just as close as Grandpa and Grandma Ruthie had been. But finally we had to admit that we had stopped making each other happy."

The words fell on Twig's head like raindrops. Too many all at once to make sense of.

"But—" Her fingers closed around a weed, twisted, and tore it out of the ground. "Dad left us. He just left."

"One of us had to go. We talked about it and decided it was better for it to be him. I'm sorry, Twig. I thought you understood that. You shouldn't be angry at him. It's not his fault."

She paused. Twig looked at the weed in her hand through brimming eyes, trying to adjust her mind so she could see things as her mother did. It was hard.

"Or maybe you should," her mother added softly. "Maybe you should be very angry at both of us."

19

Anger sat, dull and mean, on top of Twig's head.

It was like a heavy weight. It couldn't be coaxed off by one of Annie's jokes or her mother's smiles. Or by Charley licking her hand as she sat trying to do her homework, telling her that he was her dog now. It didn't wear itself out in a day or two, as anger usually did. It would not go away.

She wasn't angry at her father anymore. Well, not as much. Not so angry that he'd left, but that he'd left without saying good-bye. She couldn't be angry at her mother, despite what she had said. Her mother had been too sad for too long. Twig wasn't sure who she was angry at. The world, for being unfair? Annie's family, for being happy? But that was terrible, a bad thought. She would never want her friend to feel this way. That young couple in the wedding picture, her parents, for not knowing how their marriage would turn out?

Feelings could change. That was the awful thing, the scary thing, that her mother had told her. She didn't want to know that.

Twig stayed away from the garden. She didn't want to talk to her mother. Not right now. She stayed away from Annie's house. She couldn't bear to hear her family laugh again. She closed the door to her room and did math problems and listened to the radio and went to bed early. Charley was with her. Only Charley.

Her mother brought daily bulletins from the garden.

"Guess what?" she said, eyes sparkling. "The morning glory vines are halfway up the fence. The peas have blossoms. And Twig, your sunflowers come nearly up to my waist!"

She kept talking. She had gone back to work, bustling in and out of her office with stacks of books. She was even beginning to cook again.

Tonight she had made mashed potatoes. Or "smashed potatoes," as Twig used to call them when she was little. She had forgotten how good they were. Smooth, soft, soothing. If she kept eating them, maybe they would cover over all those sharp edges inside of her. She felt like eating mashed potatoes forever.

"Hey, this is living!" Grinning, Nathan dug into a pile that took up half his plate. "Mom, you are Wonder Woman."

It was Friday night. He was in a good mood, wearing the plaid shirt with the buttons again. He was going to visit their father, Twig was sure of it.

"Next year," her mother said, chewing thoughtfully, "maybe we'll try growing our own potatoes. I bet it's not hard." She looked over at Nathan. "What time will you be back? I wanted you to help me with that hay for the garden."

"Dad said he'd drop me off about noon."

Noon? That meant Nathan was staying overnight. Twig's anger leaped up. How could he sound so casual, as if this was the normal thing to do? And how could he stay overnight? Next thing she knew, he'd be moving out, going to live with Dad. Everything would be changed.

Nathan was looking at her. She knew what he was going to say before he even opened his mouth.

"No!" she said fiercely.

Nathan blinked. "Okay, okay," he muttered into his mashed potatoes.

After he had left, Twig stacked the plates and brought them to her mother at the sink.

"Thanks, sweetie," she said, reaching out a soapy hand to give Twig's shoulder a squeeze.

She didn't let go. Her fingers were warm. For a moment they stood that way. "You know, don't you," her mother said quietly, "that you need to see your dad."

It wasn't a question. Still, it seemed to need an

answer. Twig felt her back stiffen. She couldn't speak.

She pulled away. Her mother let her go.

"When you are ready." Her mother's voice came after her as she climbed the stairs.

The patio was covered with bright pansy faces. The last time her mother had gone to the garden center, she had brought home clay pots full of them: yellow, deep blue, dark pink. The colors were amazing. The flowers seemed to be smiling all the time. Pansies were her favorites, Twig decided.

She was sitting in a lounge chair having a drink of lemonade, recovering. Charley was curled up on the warm flagstone next to her. It wasn't clear which of them was more worn out from giving him a bath.

"You're supposed to be a water dog, you know," Twig said to him reproachfully. "You ought to like baths."

Charley lifted his head, wagging his tail as if in apology. His fur glinted gold, silky as wheat in the sun.

"Silly old dog."

It was hot for early June. Like summer. The sweet smell of blooming things hung in the air. Behind Twig, behind the circle of bushes that ringed the patio, her mother worked in the garden. She could hear her humming, but so faintly that she felt teasingly just on the edge of recognizing the tune.

Twig picked up her library book.

A car door slammed. Nathan. He was back, an hour late.

A minute later he clumped onto the patio, sneakers untied, backpack dangling from one shoulder.

"Hi."

"Hi."

This was bad, Twig thought. Neither of them knew what to say.

Nathan plunked down his backpack on a chair. "What are you drinking?" he asked.

"Lemonade. There's more in the fridge."

He banged in and out of the storm door, returning with a tall ice-filled glass. "So—" He sat down next to her. "What have you been doing?"

Twig shrugged. "Not much. I gave Charley a bath this morning."

"Great. Did he hate it? Did you hate it?"

She couldn't help smiling. "Pretty much."

"Where's Mom?"

"In the garden, of course."

He wasn't going to say anything about his visit with their father. He had decided that, she could tell. Twig picked up her mug of lemonade and held it cool against her cheek. She thought of her mother last night standing by the sink.

"How's Dad?" she asked.

"Okay," answered Nathan. He stopped, as if wondering how much to say, then plunged on. "Actually, he's good. He painted the living room so it's not purple anymore. He's thinking about moving to a bigger place. He cooked up a fantastic omelet with everything in it for breakfast. And I met Charlotte."

"Charlotte?"

"She lives downstairs. I think she's his girlfriend."

Something crashed, loud, on the flagstones. Charley jumped up, barking. Twig gazed down at her feet. Chunks of white, fragments of rabbits, a spreading puddle of wet. "My mug!" She looked at Nathan, his eyes round, mouth dropped open in surprise. Had he really just said that? This couldn't be happening. Her father. A girlfriend. Her mug that she'd had since she was a baby.

Maybe she could glue it back together. But there were so many pieces. Twig saw the blue rabbit's foot, his white puff of tail. She reached for them.

Then, spots of red dripping on white. Looking down, Twig saw blood streaming from her hand.

"Ohhh." She stared in horror.

"Here." Nathan fumbled in his backpack, pulled out a T-shirt, and wrapped it around her hand. "Come on inside. We'll wash it off. Mom!" he called.

Twig was shaking now. She couldn't look. Nathan was leading her inside. A moment later her mother was standing next to her at the sink, saying, "What happened?"

She was so very calm. Carefully she washed all the blood away until they could see that it was only her thumb that was cut. She talked to Twig in a low murmuring voice. "It's not so bad, really it's not. See? It's just a small cut, deep but clean. It's going to be okay, sweetie." Then she had Twig sit down with her hand wrapped up, putting pressure on it until the bleeding stopped. Finally she took her upstairs to the bathroom to put on a bandage.

Twig sat on the edge of the bathtub. She had sat there so many times before. For scraped knees and elbows, splinters. When she was very small, her father used to let her play with the coins in his pocket to keep her busy while he probed for a difficult splinter.

She wasn't shaking anymore. Her thumb ached in a dull way.

"This will sting for a minute." Her mother smiled. That was what she always said when she dabbed on the alcohol.

Twig took a deep breath. Her nails dug into the palm of her hand as pain washed over her.

"Now for the bandage." Her mother held them out for her to choose. When Twig was little, she always took the biggest. This time she pointed to a medium one.

Her mother carefully positioned the bandage, then wrapped it securely around. "All better," she said, kissing the thumb lightly just as she always did.

Unexpectedly, Twig began to cry.

For a long moment her mother just looked. Then her arms went hard around her. Twig's face was buried in her mother's neck. She kept crying. She couldn't stop. She would never stop.

She felt like burrowing into her mother until she found some safe place inside. Her mother was rocking her, stroking her hair. Her neck smelled like damp earth. "Oh, sweetie," she murmured, "I'm so sorry. I never meant for this to happen. I wanted us all to be happy." Maybe she was crying too. "When your dad left, it was so hard and I was so sad. You needed me, I know, and I wasn't there. I'm so terribly sorry."

Thoughts swirled in Twig's head. Her smashed mug. Her smashed life. How strange to be sitting like this on the bathtub.

"He's never," she said, choking, into her mother's shoulder, "coming back."

Her mother squeezed even tighter. "No," she whispered.

"I can't—" Twig began. But then another wave of sobs rolled over her.

Her mother's arms folded her inside.

"We can," she said.

20

"So," said Grandma Ruthie on the telephone. "Are you going white-water rafting with me?"

"Sure," Twig heard herself answer.

"What?" said her mother on the extension.

What was she doing? Twig asked herself. She hadn't made up her mind yet. She hadn't even been thinking about it. Why had that popped out of her mouth?

"Mama? What's going on? Are you up to something?"

Grandma Ruthie chuckled. "Twig will tell you. And I'll send all the details, I promise. Oh, Twig, this is going to be fun! But now I have something else to tell you both. You'll never guess what I did this morning before breakfast. I had my first ride in a hot-air balloon!"

Somehow Twig wasn't surprised. Grandma Ruthie

soaring up into bright blue sky, bobbing over hills, brushing treetops. The picture fit her perfectly.

"It was marvelous. Amazing. I can't describe the feeling. It was like riding on the wing of a giant bird. No, that's not quite it. More like being perched on a cloud. Everything is so still. You are riding on the wind, so you can't hear it or feel it. It's magical, like a dream."

"How long were you up? How did you get down?" Her mother's voice sounded worried. Strange, thought Twig, how in her family the daughters were always worrying about the mothers.

"I don't know how long we were up." Grandma Ruthie seemed still in a dream. "Maybe an hour, but it felt like forever. Oh, and the landing was such fun! We floated down, soft as a feather, right in the middle of a farmer's field. The cows watched us, their noses in the air. Have you ever seen a cow looking up at the sky? Dogs were barking, horses ran away, and finally the old farmer came moseying out of his barn. For the longest time he just stood and stared, not saying a word. Then he called to his wife, 'Martha, put the kettle on. The Martians have landed.' We all went inside and had coffee. And by the time we left, that old farmer was asking the pilot, 'How can I get a ride in one of them contraptions?'"

Twig's mother was laughing now. "Only you,

Mama," she said. "Things like this can only happen to you."

"I can't wait to go up again!" Grandma Ruthie rolled along, breathless. "Do you know there are ballooning clubs all over the country? And balloon festivals? The biggest one is in Albuquerque in October. Oh, wouldn't it be fun if we could all go!"

Surprisingly, Twig's mother didn't say no. "Maybe we will," she replied.

"Just one more thing before I go to my yoga class. Twig, are you still there? I sent you something. You should be getting it any day now."

"Me?" said Twig. "What is it, Grandma?"

"Can't tell you. But it's something special. Goodbye, you two. Take good care of that garden. And tell Nathan to run fast."

" 'Bye, Grandma."

" 'Bye, Mama. You take care."

Twig was smiling when she hung up the phone. Talking to Grandma Ruthie did that to her. It also made her feel like doing something. Maybe not going up in a hot-air balloon, but something that she hadn't tried before.

Like baking a cake.

Her other grandmother used to make a chocolate cake with raspberry jam between the layers that everyone loved. Especially Nathan. When he was little, she always made it for his birthday. Since she had died, they hadn't had that cake. But Twig knew where the recipe was, written out in Grandma Rose's tiny careful handwriting.

She would surprise him and make it for dinner. There was just time, if she started right away.

Twig got out the mixing bowl and cake pans and lined up all the ingredients on the counter. She knew more about cooking now than the first time she'd tried it. She had been watching her mother. Maybe she would put real flowers on top, like Grandma Rose used to do. Pansies! The blue and yellow ones would be perfect. Twig hummed as she mixed, thinking of Nathan's face when she set down the cake on the table.

But when she took the round pans out of the oven, her hopes fell. The cake looked so flat. Like two very large pancakes. That didn't seem right. Then she had to get the layers out of the pans. How were you supposed to lift out something so big? The recipe didn't say. Twig tried the skinny spatula, then the fat hamburger turner, then both together. Finally, just as she thought she had it, lifting one layer free of its clinging pan, the cake split right in half.

That was when her mother walked into the kitchen.

She stared, a dazed unseeing look in her eyes. It was a look she often had when she finished working. She was still in the Middle Ages.

"Oh, Mom." Twig looked down in dismay at her broken cake.

"It's okay, sweetie. We can fix it." Her mother took the spatula and hamburger turner out of her hands. She lifted one of the broken pieces onto a plate, then set the other close against it, like fitting together a puzzle. "There, see? We'll cover it with frosting, and no one will ever know. I've repaired many a cake that way."

She pinched a crumb out of the pan. "Anyway, your stomach doesn't know what it looks like. Mmm, good. Isn't this Grandma Rose's cake?"

Twig nodded glumly. "It was going to be a surprise for dinner. But I had all this trouble and now it's six o'clock and it isn't even cool yet and I still have to make the frosting."

"So?" Her mother smiled at her. "We'll have a non-surprise cake not for dinner. We can have it at midnight. Who cares, if we get to have that cake?"

She tasted another crumb. So did Twig. It really *was* good.

"Cake orgy later, then?"

"Okay," agreed Twig.

"I can't wait," said her mother, licking her fingers.

It wasn't midnight, but close to it when the cake was finally ready.

Everything else that could go wrong with it had gone wrong. The frosting had come out runny, and Twig had to keep adding sugar and then leave it in the refrigerator forever to harden. When she put the second layer on top of the first, it looked lopsided. She tried adding more raspberry jam to the side that sank down, but it oozed out all over the plate. Then, when the frosting finally seemed ready, it wasn't— and it ran down all over the plate too. The plate was a mess. The cake was still lopsided. How had Grandma Rose done it? Well, Twig told herself, their stomachs wouldn't know what it looked like.

She went outside in the dark and picked pansies to go on top. Maybe that would help. Then she went to call her mother and Nathan.

Her mother looked up from the book she was reading in the den. "Just in time," she said, yawning. "I was about to fall asleep."

From behind Nathan's door came guitar sounds. Chords, louder and surer than before, and in tune too. But low and sorrowful. She caught snatches of words. "Got me a hard-hearted woman . . . My life's one long misery . . . Goin' to the station . . . Catch the first freight train I see . . ." She never had heard Nathan sing.

He came to the door when she tapped on it, eyes blinking, tousled hair so long now that it curled around his ears. He wasn't going to cut it, she could tell. He seemed older.

"I'm learning the blues," he mumbled, looking embarrassed.

They sat around the table in the dimly lit kitchen, the three of them. And Charley, pressed against Twig's knee, hopefully eyeing the cake. It was surprising, thought Twig, how good it looked when she knew what a mess it was underneath.

It tasted wonderful. They each had a big slice with milk, and then she and Nathan had seconds, and Nathan had thirds. Twig gave Charley just a crumb, since he was on a diet again, under the table.

"I can't believe you did this," said Nathan, shaking his head. "Grandma Rose's cake. You know you're going to have to make it again for my birthday next month."

"Okay," agreed Twig, smiling.

Her mother told Nathan about Grandma Ruthie's call and her latest adventure in the sky.

"Fantastic!" Nathan grinned. "From underground caves to up in the clouds. You can't keep a good woman down. Next thing we know, she'll be orbiting the earth in a spacecraft." He raised his glass of milk. "Here's to Grandma."

Twig could see Grandma Ruthie in a space suit, doing a little skywalk just for fun. Kicking up her heels in space.

It felt as if she was there with them. They had come together again, Twig thought, her family. Like a puzzle that had been taken apart and put back together in a slightly different way. Or islands, becoming a mainland.

They clinked glasses.

"To Grandma!"

21

His voice hadn't changed.

Not a bit. "Twig," he said right away. You could hear the smile on his face.

But all Twig could hear was her heart thumping in her ear: *boom, boom, boom* like a bass drum. Why had she dialed his number? What was she going to say?

Everything had gone out of her head. She looked out the kitchen window. A yellow bird sat in a round bush. A chipmunk scurried across the patio. Looking over its shoulder to make sure the coast was clear, it climbed into a clay pot, in among the pansies, tipping up their faces. It was drinking dew from a leaf, she saw.

The concert, that was it. She took a deep breath.

"The spring concert," Twig said. "It's Wednesday night. Do you want to come?"

"Of course." He sounded pleased. "I wouldn't miss it."

Silence again. Well, that was it. That was all she had to say. She hadn't thought of what came next.

"What's on the program this time?" her father asked.

"Annie's playing a violin solo. She's been practicing like mad. I'm just in the chorus. But we get to wear these funny hats for one song. The boys' are straw and the girls' have fake fruit on them."

Now she was babbling. Twig stopped.

Another pause.

"Well, thanks for inviting me," her father said softly.

"Okay."

It seemed as if there was something else she should say.

"Oh. It's at eight o'clock."

"Great. See you then. 'Bye, Pearl."

Pearl of a girl. Twig swallowed hard. "'Bye."

She hung up the phone. Everything they hadn't said echoed inside her head. *Sorry. I love you. I miss you.*

"'Bye, Dad," she said to the empty kitchen.

22

The package was a strange shape, long and narrow.

What kind of crazy thing could Grandma Ruthie be sending her? A stalactite from a cave? An icicle from Alaska? A walrus tooth to go with her whale's tooth?

Something special, she had said. Opening the box, Twig found a small rusty shovel inside. A trowel, her mother would call it. The wooden handle, once red, was cracked and the metal tip bent back. It looked as if it had been buried in the earth for about a century.

"For digging and delving," read Grandma Ruthie's scrawled card. "This used to be Grandpa's."

Twig had to smile. Who ever heard of such an odd present? Grandma Ruthie had done it again. She was full of surprises.

She went out to the garden to show her mother.

"Oh, my." Her mother stopped staking tomato plants, reaching out a finger to touch it. "I remember that trowel so well. Grandpa always had it in his hand."

The tomato plants had gotten tall, Twig noticed. Like everything else in the garden. Sugar snap peas climbed nearly as high as her head. Morning glories twined along the top of the fence. And her sunflowers, with their hand-sized leaves, seemed on their way to becoming trees. It was hard to believe all this had come from a few seeds in the ground.

"Can I help?" she asked.

"As a matter of fact, you can put that trowel right to work," her mother said. "I want to move those two cucumber plants. They're too close together."

Twig knelt and dug into the soil. The trowel felt right in her hand. Smooth, sharp. She thought of Grandpa, his large work-worn hands holding this same trowel. She could almost see him. "Row, row, row your boat," she thought. Grandma Ruthie was right. The old rusty trowel was something special. A good gift.

"Would you look at this?" Her mother's eyes flashed excitement. "A blossom! Oh, and here's another one."

Tiny yellow starlike flowers. Twig saw them, nearly hidden in the triangle-shaped leaves.

"With a little luck, each one will become a tomato. And then what a feast we'll have!"

It was amazing. Everywhere Twig looked, suddenly, were blossoms. Beans, sugar snap peas, tomatoes. Even the morning glories on the fence had clusters of tight little buds, about to burst open. The garden seemed to be exploding as she watched.

And as she watched, a white butterfly flitted past. It zigzagged above the row of bush beans, a flutter of white against blue sky. It skimmed by her, hovered over the sugar snap peas, then finally lighted on a plump pink-white blossom. Its wings stuttered and stopped. For a long moment it hung there, motionless.

Twig felt as if she shouldn't breathe. Time stopped. The colors seemed extraordinarily bright: sky-blue, leaf-green, white. The sun so warm, the air perfectly clear. Her mother and herself, working quietly together. Grandpa's trowel digging into rich dark earth. Without looking, she felt that her mother was smiling, happy now. At this moment everything seemed right, peaceful, in place.

A flicker of wings, and it was gone. The butterfly soared up, over the sunflowers, and out of the garden.

Twig stared. It was as if it had never been. Still that feeling lingered on.

She set the second cucumber plant into its new hole, smoothing the soil around it. Unexpectedly, she said, "I talked to Dad yesterday."

"Oh?" Her mother's voice was soft in the hush.

"He's coming to the spring concert next week."

"That's good. I'm glad."

Twig looked once more at the place where the butterfly had been. Definitely, it was gone. But something else caught her eye. Something small and green and flat. Oval-shaped, but not a leaf.

She stood up to see better. "Mom," she said, "what's that?"

"What?" Her mother shaded her eyes. "Hmmm. It looks like—"

Twig saw another, hanging down from a wilted blossom.

"Pea pods!" they said together.

They grinned at each other.

"Look." Her mother pointed. "Another one."

"And one over there."

"I can't believe it. My first crop!"

They danced around, hugging. Then they poked among the strings, discovering still more.

"Eight, nine, ten," counted Twig. "Can we pick them?"

"Absolutely."

Twig made a shallow bowl out of the long end of

her T-shirt, piling them in. A dozen or more. Her mother turned on the hose.

"Here's how we used to do it, Grandpa and I," she said, smiling.

She pointed the hose up like a fountain, waved a pea pod through the gentle spray, then popped it into her mouth.

"Oh, my," she sighed, closing her eyes.

Fine drops of spray drifted down, cooling Twig's bare arms. She bit into a pea pod. It crunched. Sweetness filled her mouth. It tasted like sun and sky and earth and water and blooming things.

"This is the best pea I've ever tasted," she said. Possibly even the best taste she'd ever tasted.

"What did I tell you?" Her mother sank back, leaning against the fence. "Here, sweetie, have another one."

They sat there, eating peas and getting wet, surrounded by the garden.

Twig had the strange feeling again of time stopping, of something she ought to notice. Happiness. That was what it was. At this moment she felt completely happy. Maybe, she thought, that was all there was in the world for anyone: moments like this. She needed to remember them. Like butterflies, they flitted away.

"Hey, what's going on?"

The moment vanished. Nathan, back from his run, stood by the back door.

"Pea pods!" her mother called happily. "Come and see!"

As he walked toward the garden, she nudged Twig with a mischievous grin. Like Annie when she played tricks on her brothers. "Let's surprise him," she whispered, nodding at the hose.

Twig understood. Just as Nathan came around the forsythia bush, she let fly with a stream of water. Her aim was perfect. She caught him right in the chest.

"*Yowp!*" He yelled, surprised. Dark splotches dotted his green shirt. But then he began to grin. "That feels good. More!"

Twig pointed the hose at the sky. Like a fountain, water arced high in the air, tiny drops shimmering like crystals. The droplets floated, silvery, against deep blue sky. For just a moment they were caught by the sun, making a flash of rainbow.

Then they fell to earth, drenching all three of them.

About the Author

Jean Van Leeuwen's highly acclaimed novels for young people include *The Great Summer Camp Catastrophe*; *Dear Mom, You're Ruining My Life*; and her most recent, *Bound for Oregon* (all Dial). She is also the author of the best-selling Dial Easy-to-Read stories about Oliver and Amanda Pig, including the ALA Notable Book *Tales of Amanda Pig*. Her most recent picture book is *Across the Wide Dark Sea: The Mayflower Journey* (Dial), illustrated by Thomas B. Allen. Ms. Van Leeuwen has two grown children. She and her husband live in Chappaqua, New York.